THE ASHOKA SERIES: THE BATTLE FOR TAKSHASILA

BOOK II

VIGNESH GANESH

Made with ♥ on the Notion Press Platform
www.notionpress.com

This book is dedicated to my family and friends who believed that I could be a writer.

And a special thanks to all the Readers who have purchased this book and journeyed with me from the series' first book to this second one. You inspired me to continue writing, and I hope I can count on your continued support!

Contents

Contents

Preface

Firstly, the corrigendum. I apologise to the readers for stating that the character Khara is from Vaishali in Avanti on Page 83 of the first book. Khara is from Vaishali which is in the Vrijj confederacy. Now we can get to the preface.

As I sat down to write the second book of the series, I originally envisioned the central plot to revolve around the idea of the protagonist undertaking another adventure, beyond the borders of the Mauryan Empire. However, a particular event stood out in the overall plot that eventually proved too good and too great to be confined to a few pages of the book. That was the Battle for Takshasila.

While not much is known about the war, I have envisaged the event as a series of clandestine plots and inevitable events culminating in a battle for the ultimate prize: Ancient Takshasila which was a treasured city of the Mauryan Empire. It was the curiosity regarding the geopolitical situation in ancient Bharatvarsha and its neighbours that got me thinking about this watershed event, which is etched in our historical memories. I decided to write it as a fictional account through the common eyes of Samudra, an ordinary citizen and from the view of Prince Ashoka, the unwanted son, but accomplished son of the Emperor. It is an objective I hope to have accomplished through this book.

Samudra's role as a spectator as opposed to Ashoka's role as an aggressive actor shows how the fate of Takshasila is held hostage by the grand ambitions of great men who covet the ancient city.

Writing this book has been a journey of discovery for me. It has allowed me to explore the nuances of history and fiction as I watch them merge into a story that I hope will resonate with readers as much as it has with me. This second installment is not just a sequel to the first book, but an exploration of what was and what may have transpired in ancient India at the height of the Mauryan Empire.

So, may this tale of Ashoka, Samudra, and Takshasila transport you to the land of ancient Bharatvarsha where the eclectic mix of history and fiction blend to bring the past to life!

Thank you for joining me on this adventure.
-Vignesh Ganesh

Acknowledgements

This book is a small book, but it showed me that I had it in me to follow up and write the series of books I always envisioned for Samudra and his journeys. The story turned out very different in the first draft with a very different title and ending. But, along the way, numerous people helped me and put up with me as I spoke at length about the book's characters, the places, the events that would unfold and the changing ending.

First and foremost, I thank my parents, Sandhya and Ganesh and my sister, Aishwarya who put up with me talking about how I fictionalised the Mauryan period in India. Further, they patiently pointed out some discrepancies which hopefully have been addressed in this book draft. Thank you my family for your patience and your guidance.

Then there are my friends who kept enquiring occasionally about how the writing had progressed and where the plot had reached. They played a major role in the plot of this book moving forward and their interest in the story sustained mine. Also, I am grateful for their tips on how to amplify the reach of this book. Thank you guys for the encouragement.

I thank my extended family who constantly motivated me to write and believed that I was capable of writing my own books. Well, I hope I have upheld your beliefs and the expectations you have for me.

I especially want to thank Adithya for his wonderful foreword and his lengthy discussions with me on various historical topics.

ACKNOWLEDGEMENTS

Last but not least, thank you Notion Press for giving me this opportunity to publish my book and help me continue the series that is so close to my heart.

Foreword

In "The Battle of Takshasila", Vignesh takes us on an extraordinary journey into a world on the edge of chaos – a world where fate, ambition, and survival collide against the looming backdrop of the Battle of Takshasila. This is not just a retelling of history – it's a journey into a world that feels alive, where every decision carries the weight of a kingdom, and every moment pulses with emotion and tension.

At the center of it all is Ashoka, not yet the emperor we know, but a man discovering the depths of his strength and the limits of his ambition. Through his journey, we see the conflicts both external and internal – a battle not just for Takshasila but for identity, purpose, and the soul of a leader. With remarkable depth, Vignesh captures this timeless struggle of identity and purpose that resonates with us all, no matter the era.

What makes Vignesh's writing stand out is his unmatched ability to narrate a story which is highly cinematic where you can almost hear the clash of swords, feel the tension in the air and be immersed along with the characters on their journeys. Through his book, medieval India comes alive in ways that few have dared to imagine. Whether you are a history buff or simply someone who likes a great story, this book will draw you in with its impeccable pacing, twists and turns and genuine depth of its characters.

- Adithya Balasubramanian

List Of Characters In Alphabetical Order

Abaya: A Buddhist monk of the Kalinga Vihara and former guardian of Samudra

Ajita: An Ajivika scholar and one of the principal advisors of Emperor Bindusara

Akshaya: The son of a prosperous gems merchant in Takshasila and the best friend of Samudra

Antiochus: The second Greek emperor of the Seleucid Empire and son of Seleucus

Ashoka: The third son of Emperor Bindusara and the prince of the Mauryan Empire

Bindusara: The Mauryan Emperor of Bharatavarsha and son of Emperor Chandragupta

Buddhamitra: The abbot of the Kalinga Vihara and the teacher of Samudra

Chanakya: The first Mahamatya of the Mauryan Empire and principal advisor of Emperor Chandragupta

Chandragupta: The first emperor of the Mauryan Empire and Bharatavarsha

Deimachus: A Greek ambassador to the Mauryan Empire from the Seleucid Empire under the rule of Antiochus

Dhanavantri: A master physician from the city of Pataliputra

Gautami: A Buddhist nun and friend of Haridasa

Haridasa: A Gandharan scholar who is the Guardian Guru of Samudra in Takshasila and the husband of Varaprada

Indrabahu: A prosperous merchant of Takshasila and the chief accountant of the Takshasila Merchant Guild

Jhadamitra: A prosperous Persian merchant and former Setti of the Takshasila Merchant Guild

Khara: The Mauryan garrison captain of Takshasila

Nikaias: A Bactrian general in charge of a hostile Bactrian army

Prabhakara: A Mauryan soldier in training and a candidate for Prince Ashoka's personal guard

Radhagupta: The Amatya of the Mauryan Empire and the principal advisor of Emperor Bindusara

Samudra: An orphan boy from foreign shores adopted by Buddhist monks who have been sent to study in Takshasila under the tutelage of Haridasa and Varaprada

Seleucus: The founding emperor of the Seleucid empire and rival/father-in-law of Emperor Chandragupta

Somadeva: A prosperous horse trader of Takshasila, member of the Takshasila Merchant Guild and member of the Advisory Council of Gandhara

Sushima: The Crown Prince and the first-born son of Emperor Bindusara

Suryanaga: An influential Buddhist scholar of Gandhara and brother of Vasunaga

Vara: A Buddhist monk at the Kalinga Vihara and former guardian of Samudra

Varaprada: An esteemed scholar in Takshasila and wife of Haridasa

Vasunaga: The wealthiest man in Takshasila and de facto head of the Takshasila Merchant Guild

Prologue

As I walked through the desecrated ruins, I felt the blood-soaked earth under my feet, the overhanging red skies over my head and the fields of corpses ahead of me. The distant wails of men, the clash of swords and shields, the shrieks of fallen elephants and the screams of dying horses filled the air. My eyes scanned the scenery that lay ahead of me. Vultures feasted on the bodies of the dead and the dying. A group of women and children stood around an unrecognisable corpse and cried their hearts and cursed a long-gone or long-dead killer. A fire or two burned indiscriminately as pungent smoke displaced the life-giving air.

I found a man pushing and shoving bodies off him as he struggled for space and air with the dead. He gasped and panted for air and as he stood up, he appeared dazed. He looked around groggily when his gaze met mine. As our eyes locked, he took a step in my direction and I instinctively took a step back. As I did, I tripped and fell on something soft and warm. Something wet trickled down my face and as I wiped it away, I screamed my lungs out as I desperately tried to get the blood off my hands and pushed away the source of it, a dead body away from me. As I jumped to my feet, the man had already covered the gap between us and I got a good look at his face, I realised I was seeing the consequences of war itself inflicted upon a man. He stood dazed, unaware of his surroundings and his face was mutilated beyond recognition. Morbid wounds decorated the visible parts of his body and tatters covered the remaining. Before a word escaped his mouth, my legs carried me far away from the place.

I could not bear the thought of spending a minute more in this hellish landscape. As I ran away from the nightmare, its horrors followed me. The fields of corpses stretched as far as the eyes could see and there was no escape from the red skies that hung over the world like the shadow of death itself. In my bid to escape these horrifying sights of death, I did not notice that I was running towards the cries of savagery and misery. I was surrounded. Every moment was an assault on the senses. I had to escape this world of horrors. As I stopped running, a realisation struck me. There was no way such a place could exist in the world I knew.

As I stood still and tried to gather my thoughts, in all the gory commotion, I thought I heard the faint splash and flow of a river nearby. I made my way shakily to the river to wash my face of all the grime and dried blood and clear my thoughts. My mind was elsewhere and as I scooped up water using my hands, I recoiled in shock. The river water flowed crimson and as my eyes widened, I saw parts of dead bodies bobbing and floating in the shallow waters. The face of a child floated right in front of my eyes, staring lifelessly back at me. Those young eyes held so many questions, to which I had no answers. But then, the possessor of those eyes would never get the answers to the questions. Before I knew it, tears flowed down my eyes and as I furiously wiped them away, I looked up at the red skies, searching for any trace of divine intervention that would reverse all the mishappenings and hardships that had plagued this land. As my blurry sight cleared, I saw a train of chained men and women across the neighbouring bank being led to what appeared like a giant wheel spinning in mid-air. There were whipmen positioned at random places who inflicted corporal punishment upon the chained as they moved step by step towards the giant wheel.

It was an odd sight for though the scene was not clear, I thought I heard raucous laughter from the chained prisoners. The whipmen brutally whipped and beat them, but they kept laughing. Additionally, I had never seen such a large wheel in my life before. Its purpose was unclear and I could not even imagine the magic behind the wheel's suspension in mid-air and the force behind its movement. But, the wheel kept spinning naturally without any support, as if it was the most regular thing in the world.

Another peculiar sight caught my attention as my gaze moved from the chained people and the giant wheel.

Atop a mound of corpses was a magnificent throne with a fierce lion's head making up the throne's top at its back. The throne's feet resembled a massive lion's great paws. On both sides of the throne were armrests, with a lion standing beside each of them. The throne appeared to be made of solid gold and its frame was studded with precious gems. It was a lion's throne.

At the base of the throne was a stocky man, dressed in all the best finery wealth could afford. The man was desperately clutching to one of the standing lions beside the armrest and weeping bitterly. The throne radiated power and the man at its base, if seated upon it, would have all the power humanly possible in the world. Despite that, the man appeared unhappy beyond measure, his tears proof of his overflowing sorrow. But, on the other hand, the chained prisoners who bore every pain and atrocity meted out to them in this world, suffered with a smile and even laughter on their faces.

As I rose and walked away from the river of blood and corpses, the cruel world of war and slavery loomed large before me. Was I to live in such an unfair and unjust world?

What was my role in it? Why was I made to watch all this?

As these thoughts occupied my mind, a hand caught hold of my shoulder and dragged me away from the nightmare landscape.

I awoke with a start as I found Varaprada regarding me with concern.

"Oh, Lord Vishnu be praised. You are awake. It was getting difficult to wake you up. You were muttering in your sleep and it seems you are running a high fever. Your body is burning up."

I did not feel the heat radiating from my body, nor did I feel ill. All I felt were the burning questions left within me in the wake of the horrifying dream.

"I am sorry for worrying you. I am fine," I muttered and tried to rise from bed.

My body did not support the assurances that had escaped my mouth and I immediately collapsed to the ground.

I faintly saw Haridasa enter the room and immediately help his wife lift me and gently place me on the bed.

Varaprada was pleading with Haridasa in a worried tone and her husband received all of them with an impassive face. I did not understand the pleas due to my weak state, but I did get Haridasa's response.

"Forgive me, Varaprada, but I have got to leave. The Macedonians and Mauryans are at our gates and we have to respond."

I saw Haridasa leave the room and Varaprada slumped on the bed next to me and patted my head. As her hands gently caressed and comforted me, all my troubles and questions slipped away as I drifted to sleep again.

Elsewhere, another man's nightmares were tinged with the memories of the past. An innocent boy stood atop a barren hill as he watched the only man whom he had ever loved in his life burn before his very eyes. But the boy could not save him. So he ran away. He ran as fast and as far away as he could until he could not hear the screams of the old man who died that night.

Ashoka awoke with a start. His sheets were soaked with sweat and his body shuddered in fear. He had numbed himself to all pain and suffering when he was awake, but his dreams were a realm beyond his control. As he sat at the edge of his bed, a guard appeared in his tent.

"Your Highness, forgive me for my intrusion, but Captain Dharmasena has stated that we should resume our march. Takshasila is upon the horizon."

Ashoka shook away the stupor from the nightmare and ordered the messenger to spread the word across the army to prepare for the resumption of the march.

"I will protect your vision. Your vision of Akhanda Bharat will come true."

CHAPTER ONE

ASHOKA MEETS THE INVADERS

When Ashoka's orders were relayed by his messengers to his main forces, a wave of action swept across the camp. The respective captains of the regiments barked orders. They got their men into formation with their standard army-issued weapons and shields as the officers hurriedly had their armour fit on them and their weapons of choice handed to them.

The riders quickly jumped upon their loyal steed as the beasts neighed in fury, reflecting the energy of their masters. Ashoka's army had brought no elephants or chariots for these would only have slowed down the march to Takshasila. Therefore, he would mainly rely upon cavalry and infantry.

Like every army in the world, the Mauryans had their way of waging war. The Mauryan army was usually broken down into units comprising one elephant, one chariot, three cavalry and five infantry. The elephant had a spacious howdah placed upon its mighty back for five men which included one archer, three spearmen and the mahout for directing and controlling the elephant. Two to four horses drew a chariot with a charioteer and an elite warrior carrying a wide range of weapons from bows and arrows to clubs. Chariots were also known to have scythed wheels to wreak havoc among tightly packed infantry lines or destroy other chariots. The chariot and the elephant aimed to break enemy lines and create disorder among the ranks of the enemy. This would enable the cavalrymen and infantrymen to finish the job by charging into the enemy and inflicting defeat upon them.

The horsemen who rode well-bred horses were well-trained to wield spears, swords and shields as part of cavalry charges and close-range combat. Finally, the largest division in the Mauryan army was its infantry in terms of numbers. The infantrymen were armed with spears, swords and shields for close-range and mid-range combat. There was a separate unit of archers in the infantry armed with bows as long as an average man's height and attacked in a synchronised manner to rain a deadly shower of arrows upon the enemy lines.

The elite warriors of the chariot and cavalry divisions were armoured and usually came from aristocratic classes. They were the officers of the army and were placed in leadership positions. The soldiers of the infantry came from the lower classes of Mauryan society but had the option of climbing up the ranks to become officers in the army through merit.

Ashoka's forces never followed the conventional formations of the Mauryan military. The forces of the prince, though units of the Mauryan Crown in name, were loyal to him and were a corps of battle-hardened men who were willing to sacrifice their lives on the prince's orders. They were men who had mostly fought dacoits in the forests of central Bharatvarsha and the tiny kingdoms beyond the Vindhya mountain range. However, Ashoka's forces were known for their speed and battle tactics. His army had two commanders who were loyal to the prince. Dharmasena and Udayaditya were two sides of the same coin.

While Dharmasena came from a distinguished family of military men who had served the Mauryan Crown since its inception, Udayaditya was a first-generation soldier who had joined the army in his late teens as an infantryman. He had climbed the ranks through sheer determination and merit. Udayaditya had always been the the first man to volunteer for any mission that took him to the remotest parts of the empire including the most hostile terrain. His strength and endurance impressed his superiors and he received training from the best of the best. When Udayaditya emerged as a finely trained warrior, having proved his mettle in the most difficult of missions, the captains of the army competed with each other to recruit him with their units. Ultimately, Udayaditya joined Ashoka's forces and accompanied them wherever they were needed.

Bindusara had sought to keep Ashoka away from the comforts and political power centres in Pataliputra to prevent the prince from cultivating any real political support for himself in the capital. Due to this reason, Ashoka was sent to the remotest corners of the empire where lawless and disorderly elements reigned supreme. Ashoka and his men put down these elements and brought them to heel. After establishing Mauryan law and order in the region and handing it back to the administrators, Ashoka moved on to the next region where the orders took him. And now, the orders had brought him to Takshasila.

While Ashoka was busy with Udayaditya near the outskirts of Takshasila, Dharmasena was in charge of the main forces and their mobilisation against the enemies. As the camp was rife with chaotic activity, Dharmasena was in his tent in consultation with the captains.

"We have only received orders to be prepared for the enemy. The problem is we do not know who the enemy is," Dharmasena barked at the men.

"We received intelligence that two hundred Macedonian horsemen carrying the banners of King Antiochus entered Gandhara through the northwest. There is no confirmation on whether they are the advance force or the main force," a captain replied.

"King Antiochus would never make the mistake of sending a measly two hundred men to conquer a region that has always been a point of contention between the Yavana and Mauryan Empire. We must assume that this is an advance force. But, why are they out in the open even if it is an advance force? This must be a trap," Dharmasena opined.

"My Lord, whether it is an advance force, the main force or a trap, we must decide and act quickly for the Prince is out there. We need to ride out to protect the Prince."

"Do not worry about the Prince. He is an army unto himself. Additionally, Udayaditya is there to protect himself," Dharmasena said. "The Prince's men are enough to meet the invading force. The Prince will be safe. I shall take a thousand men and station the force at a safe distance. We will observe the interaction between Prince Ashoka's men and the Yavana men from a safe distance, ready to strike if something or someone threatens our Prince. We will relay orders over any further course of action to the remaining forces through a messenger."

The captains were apprehensive about this plan, but sensing the confidence of their commander, they agreed to the course of action.

As a thousand men, directly answerable to Dharmasena, gathered and prepared to ride behind their commander, Dharmasena barked orders to the captains who were to stay back with the remaining forces. Then, with his horse's shrill scream signalling their departure, Dharmasena led his men to back up Ashoka.

Meanwhile, a scout came to Ashoka with an urgent message stating that the Macedonian forces were approaching Takshasila.

"Are you positive that there are only two hundred men?"

"Yes, My Prince! There are two hundred men. There is no trace of a greater force hiding or following the advance force."

It was then that the realisation dawned upon Ashoka.

The Prince of the Mauryans gestured his orders to Udayaditya behind him. The Commander complied with the orders without question.

"Lower your weapons," Udayaditya barked.

The Mauryan soldiers were confused but thought better than to question the prince. They lowered their weapons and awaited further orders.

However, a shock awaited them, when Ashoka gestured for them to stay put, while he rode away. Prince Ashoka's men respected him for being the man on the front lines to lead his forces, unlike the other princes of the Mauryan lineage who rested on the laurels of their ancestors and in the comforts of the palaces.

But, this also made the prince prone to any dangers that may threaten his life. A captain came forward and whispered his doubts to Udayaditya.

"My Lord, do we let the Prince go without any backup? We have heard that the Prince is an army unto himself, but these are merely words. Even the Prince cannot cut down two hundred Yavana soldiers with their armour protecting them."

Udayaditya glared back at the captain making the officer cower.

"Do not breathe a word of this to the Prince, if you want to live. The Prince will cut you down himself if you question him on the decisions he makes. Also, he made this decision, because he believes he will not need to raise his sword at all.

Meanwhile, as Ashoka galloped across the landscape, he kept his eyes open for any potential ambushes despite his decision. Fortunately, there was no protective cover for any potential enemy to hide. Unfortunately, there was no protective cover for himself too.

As his horse sprinted through the rough terrain, he found what he sought. A large group of Macedonian horsemen were riding towards Takshasila leisurely, their flags fluttering wildly in the wind.

As soon as the Macedonians caught sight of a lone horseman on the horizon, they slowed down further and once his attire became visible to them, they came to a complete stop.

The horseman also came to a stop and stood in front of them, his posture erect and regal. His body was stocky and pockmarked, but his presence signified he was royalty. The leader of the Macedonians alighted from his horse and proceeded to prostrate himself before the prince. Ashoka was quick to descend and stop him.

"Welcome to Gandhara, Ambassador Deimachus. We have been expecting you."

"Is that why a Mauryan army awaits us at the gates of Takshasila, Your Highness," the ambassador remarked.

"It is not an army that awaits you, Ambassador Deimachus. You are a friend. It is the citizenry of Pataliputra that awaits you. We are here merely to check up on the subjects of our northwestern frontier."

The ambassador accepted this reason given by the Mauryan prince, but then sprung a surprise upon him.

"I shall enjoy the hospitality of the citizens of Takshasila first," he declared.

Ashoka cursed under his breath. If the ambassador set foot in the city, he would realise that all was well within the Mauryan empire. It did not help to know that he had no idea why the Yavana ambassador was in Gandhara when Emperor Bindusara in clear words had cancelled the ambassador's visit.

CHAPTER TWO

THE PRINCE HAS ARRIVED

Haridasa reached the Meeting Hall to find it swarming with the elites and intellectuals whose complaints resounded across the hall, leaving no room for silence. Haridasa's eyes fell upon Vasunaga, who was standing in silence and surrounded by his coterie of followers. The news of an approaching Macedonian army had made its way to the upper echelons of the city quickly.

As Haridasa navigated through the crowd, he bumped into Akshaya's father.

"Hello, Dhananjaya. How are you doing?"

"What can I say Haridasa? This entire fiasco with Somadeva is bound to hurt Takshasila's commercial standing and interests. The Merchant Guild is bound to take a beating when the whole of Bharatvarsha comes to know that the merchant who was the face of the Guild and a Councillor conspired against the Mauryan Crown and Takshasila may face punishment at the hands of Prince Ashoka or an invasion at the hands of mercenaries on the payroll of Somadeva."

Haridasa nodded in agreement and noted how Dhananjaya thought about the interests of Takshasila instead of singling out his own, unlike a few other merchants who could only think about the future of their business.

"I ask for silence from the esteemed people of Takshasila who have gathered here to discuss and decide on how to keep our city safe," Suryanaga's voice boomed across the hall.

All noise ceased as his words got the people to listen in rapt attention.

"The members of the delegation who shall welcome Prince Ashoka and put forth the perspective of Gandhara before the Prince. Any assistance required by the Prince shall be given and the perpetrators shall be punished."

Murmurs broke out again as approval of the plan spread among the people. Haridasa found himself near the podium and was immediately plucked onto the stage by the men of the assertive monk and pushed in front of the people who cheered as Haridasa stood in front of them, dumbfounded.

"With Haridasa leading the delegation, we cannot fail," Suryanaga declared to the cheers and thunderous applause of the people.

Haridasa gathered himself and stood tall. The people fell silent when it was Haridasa's turn to speak.

"Respected citizens of Takshasila, I thank you for placing your trust in me and the delegation that shall represent your interests before Prince Ashsoka. I want to assure you that I shall do everything in my power to protect the interests of Gandhara."

As the applause continued, six men consisting of three merchants and three scholars came upon the podium. Suryanaga announced their names as he declared they were members of the delegation formed under the leadership of Haridasa. The men gathered on the podium and took a vow to protect Gandhara. Haridasa acknowledged their oath and led them outside the Meeting Hall, where seven horses awaited them. The people followed them outside.

As the seven sat upon their horses, Khara and twelve Mauryan soldiers formed a protective detail around them.

"We shall accompany you and protect you from any harm to the best of our abilities," Khara said.

"We trust you, Captain Khara. Our lives are in your capable hands," Haridasa replied.

As Haridasa and his entourage prepared to leave, a woman appeared before them. Her name was Gautami and she was a well-respected Buddhist Bhikkuni and scholar among the intellectual classes. She usually spent much time outside Takshasila in places which had some connection to Lord Buddha.

"Haridasa, may I have a word?"

"Yes," Haridasa immediately complied.

Gautami took Haridasa from the group and shared with him some shocking details. She did not notice a pair of eyes trained on her.

"Haridasa, I heard about Samudra. Is he fine?"

"He is doing well, Gautami. Captain Khara saved his life."

"This is good to hear. Now for the news," Gautami said promptly. "I returned yesterday from Sanchi. I came back with a caravan of merchants from the South Gate. But along the way, I am sure that I saw Somadeva escape through the Uttarapatha in a shoddy disguise.

Haridasa's eyes grew wide with surprise.

"Are you certain that you saw Somadeva? You may be mistaken."

"I am not mistaken, Haridasa. I can recognise that man from any angle. You forget that I used to be married to him before I became a Bhikkuni."

Haridasa had to concede that bit from her. Gautami had been the daughter of a prominent merchant and high-ranking executive of the Takshasila Merchant Guild who had fixed the marriage of his daughter to Somadeva years ago after Somadeva had established himself as a top executive and member of the guild. Gautami was educated and always showed an inclination towards Buddhist studies. Gautami had immediately read Somadeva as a man of money who often thought about making money. But she also felt that he was burdened and somehow got along with him. She felt she never loved Somadeva but there was a deep understanding between them. Finally, she left the man and became a Bhikkuni with the blessings of her father and Suryanaga who held her as the newest recruit of the Buddhist Sangha in Takshasila.

Over the next few years, Gautami travelled all over the land of Jambudvipa, where she challenged numerous scholars to debates on spirituality and faith. She won some and she lost some, but she always walked away with a feeling of belonging that she never felt with Somadeva.

During her time with Somadeva, she learned to read him like the back of her hand.

Now, when she stood before Haridasa, telling him that she had seen through Somadeva's disguise and saw him escaping through the Uttarapatha, deeper into Mauryan territory instead of Bactria as he had been led to believe, Haridasa chose to believe her.

"Have you told this to anybody else?"

"I shared this news with Vasunaga yesterday itself. He said he would share it with his brother immediately, and he told me not to share this news with anybody else. But, I had to share this with you because I have a feeling that there will be no action taken on this front unless the right person knows about it."

"Are you telling me that you think Vasunaga is not the right person," Haridasa exclaimed.

"All I am telling you is that I need this information relayed to Prince Ashoka if any action is to be taken in this matter," she said with conviction.

Haridasa accepted her suggestion and promised to give this piece of information to Ashoka when he met him. As Gautami turned to leave, Haridasa uttered words of warning to the Buddhist nun.

"Hey Gautami, take care of yourself. Stay with the Sangha at all times for your safety."

The Buddhist nun smiled and left.

As Haridasa joined the others and sat on his horse, Gautami vanished into the crowd of onlookers, unaware she was being followed.

Haridasa urged his horse forward into a mild trot as the others followed him. Khara ordered his men to move along and the order was carried out. Soon they were near the South Gate when a Mauryan soldier hurriedly approached them.

"My Lord, the watchers have reported that a small company of Mauryan horsemen has been seen near the city. They are not moving and seem to be waiting for someone."

Khara was excited.

"Is Prince Ashoka with them?"

"We cannot say with confidence that he is present with them, My Lord. However, we did find Commander Udayaditya at the head of the company."

Khara was pleased with this information.

"Any sight of the Macedonian army near our gates," Khara asked immediately.

"No, My Lord. They are nowhere in sight."

"The Prince must be with the main army. Let us get you safely to Lord Udayaditya. He shall provide safe passage to you to the main camp," Khara said hopefully to the delegation members.

As soon as the words had escaped his words, cheerful roars among the sentinels standing guard on the watchtowers and the soldiers who stood guard at the massive gate below.

The members of the delegation and the detail were surprised. A loud voice came about carrying a positive message.

"Prince Ashoka has come to Takshasila. And he has brought the Macedonians along with him. They do not come as enemies, but friends."

"It seems we do not need the peace delegation anymore, Acharya," Khara said with a grin on his face to Haridasa.

However, Haridasa did not share that sentiment with Khara. Gautami's words played on his mind and an uneasy feeling rose within him.

There was never any danger to the city from foreign enemies. The enemies threatening the city's survival were within the city itself.

CHAPTER THREE

GAMES AND STRATEGY

The ambassador and his men were led by Ashoka to his war camp erected a few leagues away from the city of Takshasila. The army of Ashoka received them with ostentatious pomp and fanfare. Deimachus was put up in Ashoka's tent while his men were put up in the commanders' and captains' tents. Ashoka also did his best to arrange suitable entertainment for the ambassador before getting down to business with him. He also sent a message through a swift horseman to Pataliputra, to inform the emperor about the Yavana envoy.

The Macedonian soldiers engaged in chariot races and wrestling with the Mauryan soldiers while girls and music entertained Deimachus, a writer and a diplomat. Deimachus enjoyed himself thoroughly and cheerfully accepted the refreshments. Local delicacies and liquor flowed generously much to his delight.

Dharmasena had been thoroughly disappointed when he heard that the Macedonian force that was mistaken for an invading army was in fact, a part of a diplomatic mission. He continued to suspect Deimachus and believed the ambassador had ulterior motives other than cultural exchange. Either way, he decided to keep an eye on the Macedonian diplomat.

His mission of surveilling the Macedonians did not last long. Ashoka needed a message to be sent to Takshasila which informed the city's Mauryan garrison that the Macedonians who had arrived from Antiochus's court were friendly and would soon be on their way to Pataliputra. He had also instructed Dharmasena to explain to the administrators of the city not to breathe a word of the crisis within the city as long as the ambassador was in town. Meanwhile, if there were any concerns that Takshasila harboured, Ashoka was there to receive, address and alleviate these concerns, if it was within his power. He chose Dharmasena for this mission.

Dharmasena opposed the idea.

"My Prince, an enemy who attacks us on the battlefield must be tackled by valour and martial prowess. But, a foe that arrives under the guise of friendship must be tackled by cunning and stealth. I fear these Greeks are enemies in disguise. They are not to be believed."

Ashoka laughed heartily.

"Dharmasena, have you heard the story of the Trojan Horse," Ashoka asked the anxious Mauryan commander.

"No, My Prince."

"It is a story that Ambassador Megasthenes shared with Acharya Chanakya and the Acharya narrated to me. Your allegations against our Macedonian friends sound like that to me."

"Your Highness, Acharya Chanakya himself asserted that when a foe's intentions are unknown, we must find their motives and weaknesses to exterminate them. I am only following his teachings."

"Dharmasena, the Acharya provided these instructions for us to deal with foes, not friends. Also, Acharya Chanakya's age has ended. I saw it with my own eyes and my father ensured that. The age of enmity between the Yavanas and the Mauryans is over. My illustrious grandfather, Emperor Chandragupta Maurya ensured that. So, let me handle our foreign friends here, while you ensure we do not have any enmity with our subjects in Takshasila. Also, my response to any potential protest from you over this assigned task is that I need to send a high-ranking officer to ensure that the citizens of Takshasila do not feel slighted by the words of Prince Ashoka being conveyed to them by an ordinary messenger."

"But, My Lord..."

"Dharmasena, that is an order. You will obey," Ashoka asserted coolly. His eyes were glazed over with the promise of dire consequences hanging in every word.

After saying so, Ashoka handed over the intended message to Dharmasena for the garrison captain, which the commander fearfully accepted. Unknown to them, a pair of eyes secretly observed this exchange between the two Mauryans.

As Dharmasena left for the city to deliver the prince's message, Ashoka decided to discuss business with the ambassador and understand his motives for his sudden arrival despite Emperor Bindusara's clear message to his Yavana neighbour to the west, cancelling the visit of the ambassador.

When Ashoka entered the tent where Deimachus was placed, he was surprised to find the ambassador arranging a peculiar board with peculiar-looking beads and a pair of dice placed on the side.

"What are you doing, Ambassador Deimachus," the prince asked his guest.

"Ahha, Your Highness, I was going to send you a message to join me. Fortunately, you have come yourself. This is a board game which we Macedonians love to play. It is a strategy game called *Petteia*. I have been looking forward to a game with you."

Ashoka noted that the ambassador had been distant and sceptical about the prince's presence in Takshasila with a Mauryan army. But, once the man was sufficiently drunk, his scepticism vanished. The prince could not quite place it, but he decided to indulge the envoy from Emperor Antiochus's court.

"Well, the game looks interesting, Ambassador. However, I must seek your forgiveness, for I will not be a worthy opponent for you. I do not know the rules of this game and I will not be able to do justice to it."

The ambassador rose and stumbled to the Mauryan prince.

"Your Highness, I did not call upon you to play with me in the spirit of competition. I wanted to spend some quality time with you before I go to your eminent father in Pataliputra. Over there I shall find several worthy players who shall give me a challenge, but I may not be able to find the unique company of your presence."

Ashoka smiled, but a hint of anger gleamed in his eyes. The ambassador's words may not have held any double meaning, but his words posed a challenge to the Mauryan prince who loved winning.

"Ambassador, let us play this interesting game of yours. Kindly explain the rules of the game to me."

Deimachus scrunched his face.

"Are you certain, Your Highness? If you are not comfortable playing the game, I shall not compel you to do so. "

Ashoka was certain now that the ambassador's words were meant as an affront to his intellect.

"Let us play, Ambassador. Let the best man win."

The ambassador grinned and gestured for the Mauryan prince to sit opposite him such that they faced each other. Once Ashoka had taken his seat, the ambassador began explaining the rules. The game was played on an eight-by-eight square board with sixty-four squares. Each player was assigned beads of a particular colour. The roll of the dice determined the horizontal or vertical movement of the beads of the players. The goal of the game was for a player to surround the bead of his opponent with two of his beads and capture the opponent's bead. With the capture of the opponent's bead, the captured bead was removed from the board. If the player's beads surrounded the opponent's beads to prevent the movement of the opponent's beads or ensure the capture of all the beads of the opponent, the player would win.

The prince observed the ambassador's demeanour. The ambassador's words slurred as he explained the rules and he appeared visibly drunk, but his handling of the board was firm. Each bead was placed precisely on the board at its respective position.

"Your Highness, please roll the dice and make your move?"

The prince observed the board and rolled the dice. He made his move and awaited his opponent's move. The ambassador smiled and responded. In a few moves, Ashoka had lost his first bead.

As the game progressed, the ambassador's moves ensured that Ashoka's beads were picked out of the game. The prince smiled, realising the sobriety behind Deimachus's drunkenness.

"It seems you are a master of the game, Ambassador."

"An amateur like me can impress you because you have no knowledge about this game, Your Highness. When you understand this game, you shall realise that you play against an amateur and not a master."

Ashoka laughed.

"It seems the stories do you justice. You are erudite and a humble man.'

Deimachus laughed along with the prince and suddenly ceased. He adopted a serious tone that conveyed a warning to the prince.

"Your Highness, my beads have surrounded your beads and captured them. Sometimes, life and war play out like a game too. Sometimes, life does not tell you the rules. You should not allow yourself to be reeled in by an opponent just because a man appears to be weak or taunts you into playing his game," the ambassador said cryptically.

"What is that supposed to mean...," Ashoka asked when a Mauryan soldier entered the tent in a hurry.

"Your Highness, we have received a message from the Council of Gandhara. They shall open the gates for us and our Macedonian guests tomorrow at dawn," he informed the prince.

Ashoka turned to the ambassador, but the man struggled to keep his awareness.

"Sleep, Ambassador Deimachus. Tomorrow you shall feast in Takshasila."

CHAPTER FOUR

DREAMS OF ALEXANDRIA

As my eyes flicked open, Varaprada, who had remained by my side the whole night, touched my forehead and sighed in relief. My fever had broken and I felt much better. I tried to rise when Varaprada stopped me from doing so.

"Samudra, do not exert yourself. You need ample rest. You have not recovered completely."

I laid back weakly and took in a deep breath. I could hear the distant sound of drumbeats and trumpets but was too feeble to comprehend the reason behind the commotion.

"How are you feeling, Samudra," a familiar voice greeted me, dissipating the fog in my head to an extent. I saw Akshaya standing next to Varaprada with a large grin adorning his face.

"You seem to be better today. I heard you rolled out onto the floor yesterday. Why do you trouble the Acharya and Acharyani this way," he mocked me.

"Out of all my well-wishers, why is it that the Sun has directed you to my room this morning," I snapped back, my head throbbing in pain at the loud noise outside.

"Lord Surya has been kind to you to show you my face. If what I heard about your night mumblings were true, you seem to have imagined demons."

"My head hurt in the dreams due to the cries of the damned and it hurts now due to the commotion outside. What is happening outside," I snapped irritably.

Akshaya's grin grew broader.

"The city is welcoming the third son of Emperor Bindusara and the one whom this city was fearful of a few days ago," Akshaya said cheerfully.

"Prince Ashoka is in Takshasila? When did this happen?"

"He entered the city along with the Macedonian ambassador of Emperor Antiochus of the West in a victorious procession. He does not look anything like what I imagined."

"What did you think he would look like?"

"I thought he would be a well-built and towering man dressed in finery who would enter the city riding upon an elephant and oozing royalty. Instead, he looked like a common soldier, riding on a horse and simply nodding to the citizens of Takshasila. The Macedonian Ambassador was better dressed and more energetic than the Mauryan Prince."

"Never judge a man by his appearance and never criticise the powerful aloud," I said weakly.

"I know," Akshaya remarked. "The golden words of wisdom uttered by our Acharya who taught us Samskritam."

I nodded and tried to sit up against Varaprada's wishes. Akshaya helped me sit up.

"You two continue talking to each other. I need to complete my treatise on the Brihadaranyaka Upanishad,"

Varaprada said.

"Another treatise on an Upanishad? How many do you plan on writing," Akshaya exclaimed.

Varaprada laughed.

"Akshaya, the Upanishads are the results of mostly male authors discussing and debating among themselves with a few contributions from women. I am merely trying to understand and spread their message from a woman's perspective."

Akshaya folded his hands and bowed slowly in front of Varaprada. The Acharyani returned the favour by mock blessing him and walked away, laughing.

"You were telling me about the Macedonian Ambassador. Continue."

"Well, his name is Deimachus from Macedonia. He is a well-known poet and diplomat. During the Diadochi Wars, when the Macedonian Greek empires were at each other's throats, Deimachus was one of the few people from King Antiochus's Court who could still travel to Alexandria unharmed and was welcomed by King Ptolemy in Egypt."

"Alexandria," I exclaimed, mustering all my energy to move closer to my friend. "He has unhindered access to Alexandria!"

I nearly fell off when Akshaya caught hold of me.

"I was the fool who couldn't keep my mouth shut. How could I forget your obsession with Alexandria!"

"Why are you blaming yourself? All I want to see are the fluttering sails of all the ships belonging to every known nation in the World parked in its port."

"You came from a place where ships are sent to frequent the most tumultuous of seas in a season where the stormy skies and violent seas seek to lead ships to their watery grave. What is so great in that? If you want, my father will show you his great ships frequenting the River Sindhu," Akshaya retorted.

"There is a majestic lighthouse with a fiery crown that burns all day and night long, leading lost ships to the safety of the shore," I said dreamily.

"We have lighthouses that dot every port that in turn dot the long eastern and western coastlines of Bharatvarsha. What is so novel about Alexandria's Lighthouse," Akshaya asked in a matter-of-fact tone.

"It has a massive library full of books containing books from all over the…"

"The libraries of Gandhara…" Akshaya interjected.

"I just want to visit the city, Akshaya. I do not want to live there. Why are you trying to dissuade me," I asked him exasperatedly.

"You forget that we do not live in peaceful times. While your dreams lie in the safety of your head, your body longs to go to a place that may prove treacherous and unwelcome. You are not a diplomat or a sovereign who shall have the protection of royal soldiers."

"You forget that I am Samudra. I survived the very treacherous waters that you spoke of some time ago. I was raised and protected by people who were strangers to me. And today, I reside in the educational centre of the Known World. If it is in my destiny, I shall make it to Alexandria with the protection of our Creator. He shall write our fate, until then, I will dream," I declared seriously.

Just then, the shrill neigh of a horse was heard outside. Varaprada reached the doorstep within minutes and found a surprising guest waiting outside.

After he introduced himself, she let him in excitedly and left him in my room.

"Samudra, look who has come to visit you," she remarked.

The moment I laid my eyes on the guest, the years vanished and tears streamed down my face.

Dharmasena stood in front of me like a mountain, his hard-lined face sporting a boisterous grin.

CHAPTER FIVE

NEWS ABOUT THE FUGITIVE SOMADEVA

Seeing Dharmasena in front of me opened the floodgates and memories came flashing back in one go. Nostalgia filled me to the brim. I could not stop the overflowing tears.

"You are as frail as I remember you. You are a little taller, but otherwise, there are no changes. You need a little meat in your diet," he thundered.

Akshaya was taken aback by the boisterous stranger who stood towering in front of him.

"Is he that merchant Dhananjaya's son," Dharmasena remarked after curiously regarding the short plump youth who regarded him back with equal curiosity.

"How did you know," he blurted out in shock.

"You are a splitting image of that chubby merchant. Seen him a couple of times here and there. I never forget a face when I see one.

Also, I met a man named Haridasa yesterday. By a curious twist of fate, he turned out to be your teacher and guardian in this city. We had a small chat and here I am," he growled and laughed uproariously.

This sudden introduction of events made no sense to me, but I was mindful enough to introduce the two.

"Akshaya, this is Captain Dharmasena, a high-ranking officer in the service of Prince Ashoka."

"I am a Commander, boy. Get your facts corrected," he jabbed, taking a menacing step towards me.

For a moment, my weakness deserted my body and I nearly jumped out of bed.

Instead, he placed a hand over my shoulder and held out a message written on a palm leaf for me in his other large hand.

"What is this," I asked, as I took the leaf gently.

"I promised Acharya Dhruva that I would get this message to you. This palm leaf has travelled from Kalinga to this outpost of the Empire," Dharmasena gloated.

"You met Acharya Buddhamitra. When did this happen," I asked, deflating his inflated chest immediately.

"I saw him a couple of months ago," the commander informed me gloomily. "He appears healthy and hopes that your education is going well."

My face lit up with a smile and then grew grim with a frown.

"Wait, what do you mean he appears healthy? Either he is healthy or he is not healthy. Also, it took him four years to reach out to me? He did not even bid me farewell when he left me here," I groaned.

Dharmasena patted my shoulder.

"He was not always like this, Samudra. Once upon a time, he was a man deeply attached to the people he loved and was never afraid to show it. He is a brilliant man who was the deputy of Emperor Bindusara's Chief Advisor,

Radhagupta. He is a great man and a noble teacher. But, something happened that made him distant and...detached."

This piqued my curiosity. When I was with the abbot, I had always wondered about his past. How did a man of such a high position in the Mauryan Court become an abbot in a Buddhist vihara in Kalinga?

"What happened, Lord Dharmasena? Why did the Abbot become like this?"

The giant of a man sighed and started reciting the account of the abbot's past.

"Acharya Dhruva was born in Magadha to an advisor of Emperor Chandragupta and immediately caught the eye of Acharya Chanakya, the Mahamatya of Emperor Chandragupta, with his brilliance in childhood. He was one of the few children whose education was overseen by Acharya Chanakya and when he was old enough, he was sent to Takshasila for studies. He made friends here, probably including your Haridasa. He was the most brilliant of his guru's students and returned to find Emperor Chandragupta had abdicated his throne in favour of his son, Bindusara."

Varaprada brought some breakfast and beverages for us and went back to her treatise.

"Acharya Chanakya was not happy with the decision because he felt that Emperor Bindusara was not prepared to ascend the throne, but the first Mauryan Emperor decided it was time and left with Acharya Bhadrabahu of the Jaina Sangha to Dakshina Bharata. Emperor Bindusara never got along with Acharya Chanakya and it was under these circumstances that Acharya Dhruva returned to the Mauryan Court."

I cast a glance at Akshaya who was engrossed in a tale about a person whose ties with Takshasila were in the past and whose present path had never crossed that of my best friend.

"When your beloved Abbot returned to Magadha, Acharya Chanakya, who had his position at court given to Mahamatya Radhagupta, another of the former's students, got Dhruva the position of the Chief Advisor's deputy. It was good for some time, then some foreign businessmen came calling and Acharya Dhruva...changed," Dharmasena uttered with a scowl on his face.

Just then, I heard Haridasa's voice calling out for me. When he entered my room, he was surprised by the Mauryan commander seated along with Akshaya and me.

"Lord Dharmasena, I thought you had left with Prince Ashoka to meet the Governor," Haridasa exclaimed.

The giant rose and greeted my guardian with folded hands.

"Pranaam Panditji, I have come here to visit my old friend, Samudra. The Governor is Prince Ashoka's responsibility. As for getting close to Prince Ashoka, I am afraid it is not that easy," Dharmasena replied defensively.

"I was just asking. Forgive me if I sounded intrusive," Haridasa immediately said apologetically. "I was trying to talk to you and Prince Ashoka in the meeting, but the Councillors hogged all his time. And Deimachus kept me busy with debates and discussion. I did not want to seem impolite to the Ambassador."

The two men faced each other awkwardly until Akshaya broke the tension with his question.

"Do we get to see Prince Ashoka," he asked excitedly.

Dharmasena immediately jumped in to answer.

"Prince Ashoka is a busy man. If everything goes well without incident, there is a chance."

"What does that mean," Akshaya inquired with narrowed eyes. "The Councillor Somadeva has fled Takshasila and Prince Ashoka has successfully entered the city with the Greeks. What more could happen?"

"There is something suspicious going on in this city," Dharmasena hissed. "I can feel it in my guts. There is something suspicious about those Yavanas, especially that Ambassador, Deimachus."

"I agree," Haridasa seconded. "I was given some information by a peer of mine named Gautami. Several years ago, she was married to Somadeva and she said she saw him in disguise near the Southern Gate."

Dharmasena gawked at the scholar.

"Why did you not share this information with us? Where is this Gautami?"

"I was told that Somadeva may have escaped to Bactria. Does he intend to travel to Bactria in a roundabout fashion," Akshaya weighed in.

"Shut up, boy," Dharmasena commanded. "Now is not the time for your childish assumptions. Acharya Haridasa, I need you to come with me. Tell me everything you know about Somadeva and the people related to him. Everything that has happened so far. I need you to take me to Gautami."

"She is a resident of the Eastern Section of the city. She lives with the other Buddhist monks and nuns in the living quarters provided near the Meeting Hall."

Before I knew it, the Mauryan commander was dragging my guardian despite the Brahmana's protests. Akshaya was shocked as if struck by lightning. I waited for my friend to resume his composure to get more information on Deimachus. If there was anyone who could tell me more about Alexandria, it was the Yavana Ambassador. But, that was not to happen.

"Akshaya, do not take Dharmasena's words to heart. He is a hard man to deal with, but once you get to know him, you will know that he is a good man."

"I will also get going, Samudra. I need to check up on something with Father. Take care of yourself," Akshaya said to me suddenly, his being possessed by a mysterious feeling.

He too left in a hurry. I was left all alone seated on my bed and shrugged my shoulders in resignation. The adventures in Alexandria would have to wait while the events in Takshasila were still afoot.

CHAPTER SIX

THE ATTACK ON GAUTAMI

"You have an impressive house. I must say it is very well furnished with ample space and light. And what is that fragrance in the air," Ashoka asked as he eyed the wide assortment of Gandharan dishes placed before him.

"It is an import from Arabia. It is getting popular here. Of course, it can never replace jasmine, but I believe it is here to stay," Indrabahu declared proudly.

"It is the fragrance from Frankincense, an aromatic resin that grows in parts of Africa and India too," the Macedonian ambassador chimed in as he munched loudly on a Gandharan delicacy stuffed in his mouth.

Indrabahu smiled genially but wondered about the manners of the envoy. Deimachus, unaware of these thoughts, was munching contentedly on the delicacy.

Ashoka picked one and gingerly bit into a sweet delicacy. It melted in his mouth immediately.

Ashoka and Deimachus were invited for a feast at Indrabahu's mansion in the northern section of the city. Ashoka was sceptical about the hospitality of the merchant but accepted the invitation out of politeness.

"A great thinker named Herodotus wrote about Frankincense. He wrote that the tree from which the resin was derived was guarded by winged serpents."

Indrabahu gawked at Deimachus as he tried another dish and washed it down with wine.

Ashoka regarded the Macedonian envoy closely. Unlike the few ambassadors from other kingdoms who had visited the Mauryan court, Deimachus displayed no formality when he first entered Mauryan lands and had grown remarkably friendly within a day of his entrance into the city. He had even debated the similarities between the Greek demigod Heracles and the Indian deity, Vasudeva, with Haridasa.

"You are an interesting man, Ambassador Deimachus," a voice from a corner hissed.

Deimachus was surprised and turned to the source.

"He talks. The Merchant Prince talks," Deimachus remarked as his attention was drawn to Vasunaga.

Ashoka too was surprised. He had nearly forgotten that Vasunaga too was seated as a host, but in a corner away from the main host and guests. Until now, he seemed to be a mute spectator to the interaction between the host and guests. It made the Mauryan prince uneasy.

Vasunaga awarded the Macedonian with a rare crooked grin and rose to join his host. His grin lacked the warmth of Indrabahu but did show that the man was capable of smiling.

"Are you planning to visit Alexandria shortly, Ambassador," Vasunaga groaned.

"I plan to visit Alexandria someday when my visit and purpose of sta is done here. I shall negotiate a peace treaty with Emperor Ptolemy on behalf of King Antiochus. But for noww, I shall enjoy the hospitality of Takshasila."

Vasunaga nodded and took a seat close to his colleague, Indrabahu.

Deimachus ate heartily while Ashoka ate cautiously. Servants brought trays of various dishes, each of which was sampled by the guests. Thoroughly satisfied, the guests finally rose to wash their hands in a gold basin of water provided to them.

After exchanging a few more pleasantries and making small talk, Ashoka informed his soldiers that they were leaving. Deimachus signalled the same to his Macedonian bodyguards.

"Where are we heading next, Your Highness," Deimachus asked as the party prepared to leave.

"First we shall head to the Governor's Palace where I shall leave you and then I am heading to Haridasa's house to enjoy his hospitality."

Indrabahu was horrified.

"Your Highness, a man of your esteemed station is visiting a humble teacher's house?"

"Lord Indrabahu, Acharya Haridasa was esteemed enough to represent the city and lead a delegation to pay homage to me. Now suddenly he is a humble teacher? I thank you for feeding my soldiers and me, but I believe the Acharya's wish shall also be granted," Ashoka reverted in a sharp tone.

"Forgive me, Your Highness, I didn't mean to offend you," Indrabahu responded, flustered.

The train of dignitaries and soldiers soon left the mansion and just like that the large mansion fell silent.

The servants began clearing the dining area and Indrabahu dropped his mask of courtesy.

"Vasunaga, what is happening? This does not bode well on our plans," Indrabahu seethed.

"Hold your tongue, Indrabahu," Vasunaga whispered as he gestured to the servants.

Once the servants left, he resumed.

"You wear your emotions on your sleeve, Indrabahu. I did not take you to be impulsive like Somadeva. Prince Ashoka is free to visit whomever he wants and Ambassador Deimachus has a right to our hospitality. So let us continue our hospitality until he is not around anymore to enjoy it."

As Prince Ashoka and Ambassador Deimachus made their way to the Governor's Palace, the Macedonian envoy suffered an uncomfortable silence from the Mauryan prince. The citizens on the way bowed down to the prince's party as it made its way to Haridasa's house and Ashoka greeted them with a sharp nod without uttering a word. Deimachus decided to break the silence.

"Your Highness, I have heard that Takshasila is a vibrant city, full of raucous vigour. I do not see any of the vigour now. It seems as if the city is unusually calm and its energy seems suppressed. Is something wrong," the ambassador asked innocently.

Ashoka squirmed. He was wondering when the restless Yavana would bring up the question. During the festivities at the camp, Ashoka had explained that he was in Gandhara as the Mauryan emperor's representative. He was merely here to ensure all was well in the Mauryan empire's northwest frontier. When he had insisted that the ambassador make his way to Pataliputra, the ambassador scoffed and brushed aside the prince's suggestion.

"Well, Ambassador, while the subjects of Gandhara are happy under Mauryan rule, they did not foresee a surprise visit from their Prince. For that reason, they are still coming to terms with my visit."

"It seems almost as if they fear you for some reason," the ambassador remarked.

Ashoka brought the horse to a sharp halt. The whole party stopped dead in its tracks.

"Ambassador Deimachus, if something is wrong in Takshasila, I shall fix it. If they love me, it is good for me. If they fear me, so be it. Either way, I do not understand why are you raising corollary questions when I have already answered the main question," the prince growled, the thread of his patience close to snapping.

The ambassador immediately backed away. The tone of Ashoka sent a shiver down the Macedonian's spine and he realised that the prince was not a man to be trifled with. He understood that it was possible that if the prince lost his patience, the consequences would be dire and fatal.

Sensing that he had bought the silence of the ambassador, Ashoka resumed his ride, with the ambassador lagging at a safe distance. As they entered the central section of the city, they witnessed a raucous commotion as a large crowd of people gathered at the corner of a street.

"What is going on here," bellowed a Mauryan guard with Ashoka.

The confusion ceased and the crowd immediately dispersed to reveal a mountain of a man who had caught hold of another man and was slapping him senselessly. His accomplice, a middle-aged man stood in a corner defending a woman as they stood at a safe distance.

Ashoka immediately alighted from the horse and made his way to the centre of the crowd in quick strides.

"Dharmasena, what is going on here? Why are you striking that man?"

Dharmasena immediately stopped attacking the man but held him securely by the neck.

"My Prince, I did not expect you here."

"Who is this man, Dharmasena," the prince commanded aggressively.

"I found this man tailing Acharyani Gautami, a friend of Acharya Haridasa. I suspect he was going to attack her in the crowd and flee."

Ashoka looked around and found Gautami hiding behind Haridasa, who had yet to abandon his protective stance.

"Take him to the garrison. We shall question him there. And call all the Mauryan officers in the city to the garrison. I want to know how Takshasila fell into such a state of lawlessness," Ashoka barked his orders.

The soldiers immediately scrambled into action to fulfil the orders. Dharmasena released the suspected assailant into the custody of two soldiers who were tasked to take him to the garrison. Ashoka marched to Haridasa and Gautami. The woman shrunk as Haridasa took a step back.

"Acharya, I request you and the Acharyani to come with us to the garrison. She will not be harmed over there. I just wish to get my facts in order and know what happened."

Haridasa turned towards Gautami and after a momentary hesitation, she nodded her approval.

"Well, Acharya, I was going to take up your offer of hospitality, but it seems that the time for hospitality has ended," Ashoka said solemnly.

All the Brahmana could do was nod dismally in return.

CHAPTER SEVEN

THE MESSENGER OF VASUNAGA

"Guruma, may I ask you a question," I cried, trying to make myself heard.

I felt much better from the care and affection that Acharyani Varaprada had showered upon me.

Varaprada immediately appeared before me and sat by my side.

"What is it, my dear," Varaprada asked affectionately. "Do you want something?"

"Guruma, why is it that the country of Bactria is so important? Why would Councillor Somadeva choose to go there? Do you have any idea about these things?"

"Oh, Bactria is possibly one of the most important neighbours and trading partners of Gandhara. Councillor Somadeva was the representative of the Takshasila Merchant Guild to Bactria. He controlled the import of horses into Bharatvarsha from the northwest and supplied them to the local Mauryan garrisons. Other merchants from the other great cities of the Ganga plains like Mathura, Ujjain, Vidhisha and Kaushambi also purchased horses from Somadeva, making him extremely wealthy. These merchants, in turn, ensured the supply of horses to the whole of Bharatvarsha. It seems he was also involved in the import of minor items like Greek figs, grapes and wine from Bactria. For this reason, he has numerous allies in Bactria."

"That would make Councillor Somadeva one of the most prosperous men in Gandhara, right," I asked.

"Yes, that made him the wealthiest man in Northern Bharatvarsha," Varaprada added.

"Have you ever met Somadeva?"

"I have only seen him from far, Samudra. But, why are you asking me this?"

"A thought just entered my mind. Why would a man who had riches beyond measure, decide to destroy the very system that allowed him to hoard such wealth."

"People like Somadeva, when bestowed with immense wealth, are never content with that. They always attempt schemes which serve to increase their wealth and power. Also, you ask this because you know Somadeva is guilty, but when Somadeva committed these transgressions, he did not believe he would get caught."

As we were discussing Somadeva and his connections to Bactria, unbeknownst to us, away from the mighty Sindhu and across the expansive Himalayas, at the foothills of the Hindu Kush mountains, there lay a sprawling war camp of four thousand soldiers comprised of numerous races like the Greeks, Bactrians, Persians, Tokhari, Sakas Parthian and warriors from several other tribes. Large mules and Bactrian camels with their twin humps were loaded with military rations and other supplies for the army's use. Several foreign languages from alien tongues resounded around the camp with soldiers sharpening their weapons, sparring with each other and riding around the camp shooting strawmen for target practice. The officers of the army themselves belonged to the different tribes inhabiting Bactria, their allegiance to one man named Nikaias.

Nikaias was one of the top generals under the Bactrian King whose aim was to see Bactria free from the status of being dominion to the greater Greek empire of Antiochus. Nikaias had visited Gandhara several years ago when he was a captain. He was a part of a Bactrian delegation as a bodyguard to the Bactrian ambassador to that Mauryan region. He had witnessed firsthand the politics of the scene, the equation between the governor and his councillors, how a few guilds were the power behind the administration of the region and how they silently resisted their Mauryan overlords.

The entire de facto administration revolved around one man, a newly minted merchant prince who expressly rejected the position of Setti in the dominant merchant guild, but silently revelled in the power that the sacrifice of that position afforded him in the guild. While the other members of the Bactrian delegation had fawned over the impotent governor for trade concessions, he had closely observed the merchant prince stealthily encroach on the governor's power through his puppet councillors. Oddly enough, a rookie Greek diplomat was unofficially in Gandhara at that time to enjoy his stay in Takshasila.

The Bactrian general ended up staying in Takshasila for a year where the Bactrian ambassador managed to secure significant trade concessions from the governor. When Nikaias was in Gandhara with the Bactrian ambassador, Somadeva was in Bactria negotiating the supply of horses to India for a handsome sum of money every year.

While the export of horses from Bactria to India had the blessing of the Greek empire, the money from the sale of horses was to flow into the coffers of the Greek emperor. But, the Bactrian nobles who served the Bactrian Satrap, Patrocles knew how to siphon off money from the treasury and had sneakily withheld a significant amount from the Greeks. It was not very different from the relationship between Gandhara and the Mauryans. That day was fast coming when Bactria would rebel and succeed in overthrowing its Macedonian Greek overlords. Patrocles had been loyal to Seleucus and was now loyal to his son, Antiochus. But, the Greek world was rife with conflict and Patrocles had been sent to the other of Antiochus's expansive empire on a campaign. This gave the Bactrian nobles and generals time to build their power. One day, they would seize freedom when the Greeks were weakened.

However, Nikaias was considered an outcast among the Bactrians for his eccentricities in recruiting warriors from the 'barbarian tribes' like the Torakhi, Parthian and Saka to bolster his forces. Greco-Bactrians and Persian-Bactrians both believed that tribesmen who lived on the fringes of Persia and Bactria were barbarians, out to barbarize the sophisticated and advanced Greek world. But, Nikaias did not care for their opinions about him. They needed the strength of his arms, but he did not need them. If Bactria was not the place where he belonged, he would carve out a place for himself elsewhere. For Nikaias that place was Gandhara. All the great conquerors of the world eyed the great city of Takshasila. He aimed to take it.

While Nikaias was pouring over the maps to lead his army into Gandhara, a captain entered his tent with troubling news.

"My Lord, a messenger comes with urgent tidings from Takshasila. He says he shall talk only with you."

"Send him in at once," Nikaias commanded. Any news from Takshasila was welcome.

The messenger walked into the tent of the Bactrian general and stood proud. Nikaias, seeing his attire immediately raised his guard and realised that the man before him was not an ordinary messenger.

"I come from Takshasila. My patron wishes to inform you that the third prince of the Mauryans named Ashoka has landed in Takshasila with a three-thousand-strong army. Your forces when combined with that of the master totals up five thousand. But, he is not to be underestimated for he is a seasoned general and warrior."

Nikaias frowned. Then a grin spread on his face. The sentinels who stood guard outside his tent took a little peek inside the tent and went back to guard duty.

"That is the way it should be done. It would be no fun if I marched upon Gandhara and there was no resistance."

"Prince Ashoka is not a boy. Further, he may be supported by a Greek unit of two hundred soldiers who will add to his forces."

"I do not know why the Greeks are there. They may want to raise support from the Mauryan Empire to help Emperor Antiochus combat Emperor Ptolemy's forces in Syria. Either way, they will merely sit and watch. They too want Gandhara. Something tells me they will not act against me. But, even if they do choose to fight us, your master can neutralise them before the great battle."

Nikaias immediately called a sentinel in and barked some orders in Bactrian to him. The sentinel bowed low and immediately set out to fulfil his task.

"You are preparing to march before the decided time based on this information given to you by a stranger," the messenger remarked in fluent Greek.

"You understand Bactrian and speak Greek," Nikaias asked with a raised eyebrow.

"I speak five languages and understand seven. Bactrian is one of the languages I understand."

"Your master has an eye for great talent," the Bactrian general praised the messenger.

"He also has an eye for whom he makes alliances, but the pass you are going to use is treacherous and filled with deep gorges and awning stretches. I almost lost my horse there to bandits. My men suffered over there."

"You are strong and smart, but you need not worry about the bandits. Their kin are soldiers in my army. We can arrive at a suitable arrangement for sharing loot, if any, from Takshasila."

The messenger immediately revealed a concealed dagger and brandished it with surprising speed and ferocity. Before Nikaias knew what had happened, the blade of the dagger drew a drop of blood from his throat.

"The alliance was made on the premise that Takshasila remains untouched. If we have a problem here, I shall slit your throat and snatch your life away. If my life is forfeited due to that, so be it."

A menacing grin spread on the face of Nikaias as he held his dagger near the gut of the messenger. His body had acted reflexively.

"Do not take everything so seriously. We can always loot the cities outside Gandhara. I assume your master shall take no offence to that."

The messenger lowered his dagger as Nikaias withdrew his blade.

"He is not my master. Merely my patron. You will not be touching any city. If the bandits cannot be persuaded by words, they will fall to blades."

"You are a trained soldier by the way you move. The man in Gandhara has recruited a gem."

"I am not a precious gem in his treasure chest. I am merely a sword in his armoury."

"Well, what is the name of the servant who serves his master so loyally and where does he come from?"

"I am not obliged to answer your questions, but know that despite wearing the attire of the Mauryans, I despise them from the bottom of my heart."

CHAPTER EIGHT

THE INTERROGATION

Gautami's stalker was bound to a pole in a prison in the garrison and beaten mercilessly, but he had not breathed a word about his plans for her.

Dharmasena was livid with anger and personally rained blows upon his helpless captive. Ashoka sat with Haridasa and Gautami, questioning them gently on what had occurred.

"I was visiting Haridasa's house to share some information with him. When I was near the bazaar in the Central Section of the city, a woman behind me screamed because the man who is in there now pushed her aside and rushed towards me. Fortunately, the place was crowded and a few people came between me and the man. He was screaming something intelligible and trying to cut through the crowd," Gautami sobbed.

"Have you seen the man inside before this terrible incident," Ashoka enquired, his eyes scrutinizing Gautami's emotions reflected on her features.

"No, this is the first time in my life that I am seeing this man," Gautami snivelled. "My teachers at the Vihara would be disappointed with me. I am a mess."

Gautami took a deep breath and brought her emotions under control. Haridasa was quiet throughout the question-and-answer session.

"Ok, how did Dharmasena and Pandit Haridasa find you?"

"They did not find me. Fortunately for me, they were in the area. The man had unsheathed a dagger and was approaching me. But he pushed me to a side and kept shouting and screaming at me. That is when Lord Dharmasena came out of nowhere and tackled my attacker. Soon, he disarmed him and started questioning him."

"What did you want to tell Haridasa," Ashoka asked with some urgency in his voice.

Gautami suddenly became alert.

"The person named Somadeva whom you have been searching for is not in Bactria as you people think. He did not escape through the Western Gate or the Northern Gate as his dead servant would have you believe. The man escaped through the Southern Gate of the city and is in Bharatvarsha. He was disguised, but I knew it was him. I was coming back from Bodh Gaya."

Ashoka gritted his teeth as he heard this news.

"Are you certain that you saw him? You say he was in disguise. It may have been somebody else."

"I was married to Somadeva for years. I can never forget him or what he looks like," she asserted confidently.

Ashoka was taken aback by her confidence.

"What is so memorable about him that you remember him and can see through his disguise too?"

"I belonged to a prosperous merchant family myself. My father was a prosperous member of the Takshasila Merchant Guild. I was betrothed and soon married to him when his influence in the Guild grew after Setti Jhadamitra's death. There is a large age gap between us and we never had any marital relations for I was always academically and spiritually oriented and he was a man who pursued material endeavours. But..."

"But what," Ashoka urged.

"But, I had never understood anyone as clearly in my life before. His habits, his motivation, his ambition, his mistakes, his secrets, his life, I knew and understood them all. He did hide the greatest secret of his life and never shared it with others. He even said so to me. But every other secret of his life was known to me. For some reason, I became his closest confidant."

"Did you trust him?"

Dharmasena's voice continuously poured out of the prison, asking questions which were met with silence from the suspect. The occasional grunt of pain escaped the man's lips, but he remained resolute on not divulging any answers.

"I did not need to trust him. I may not have known the greatest secret of his life but I knew the feelings of guilt behind it. He never had any love for me and yet he laid his soul bare to me."

Ashoka processed this revelation.

"Why did you leave him?"

"As I mentioned before, I had an academic and spiritual bent in mind. Somedeva was close to Acharya Suryanaga due to his ties with Lord Vasunaga. After interacting with me, Acharya merely suggested that I renounce my life and live as a Buddhist ascetic. I was overjoyed and implored the esteemed Acharya to accept me as a disciple. Further, I urged the Acharya to convince my father and husband to let me go.

My father needed some convincing, but Somadeva was steadfast that he would not let me go. It took Lord Vasunaga's intervention to convince my husband to let me go. Then, I formally joined the Sangha as a Bhikkuni and have been trying to achieve enlightenment ever since."

"Do you think your former husband has orchestrated an assassination attempt on the Mauryan Governor and committed treasonous acts against the Mauryan Crown," Ashoka asked in a low voice.

This question put Gautami in deep thought.

"Frankly, I believe that Somadeva is very reckless and money-minded, but I always believed that Lord Vasunaga was the power behind my husband."

"You have renounced the world. You call yourself a Bhikkuni and a member of the Buddhist Sangha. And yet you refer to Somadeva as your husband. You say you never loved him, but you know him inside out," Ashoka hissed.

"Why did you reveal this information to us? Is it because you wanted him caught, or did you want to project him as an innocent man scapegoated as the mastermind of a devious plot against the Mauryan Crown by another?"

Haridasa and Gautami were stunned by the sudden hostility displayed by the prince. He seemed an altogether different person. Just then the officers of the Mauryan garrison presented themselves before the prince.

"It was great of you to join us at this crucial time. I am grateful," Ashoka remarked sarcastically.

The uncomfortable officers grew embarrassed and squirmed in front of him.

"How does a great city like Takshasila face such a crisis of law and order," Ashoka growled.

"Assailants are openly attacking the common citizens on the street in broad daylight. The Governor is not safe in his own house from his servants. Prisoners are poisoned and killed right under our noses. Criminals brutally kill Mauryan soldiers in an all-out brawl in front of the entire city without any inhibitions. Suspects walk out of the city undetected and nobody knows anything about it. How did it get so bad," Ashoka growled

The officers trembled in front of the livid prince who glared at them with unveiled fury. Not a word escaped their mouth.

Something suddenly caught Ashoka's attention.

"Where is Captain Khara? Why is he not here?"

Nobody had any answers for the prince.

"Where is he," the enraged prince shouted.

"He left with some soldiers immediately after you arrived, Your Highness. He said he had something urgent to check."

"What urgency was that," Ashoka asked, his suspicions aroused.

"We did not ask, Your Highness," an officer replied bashfully.

Ashoka heard the snide remarks of his father in his head. The emperor would sarcastically congratulate him on his incompetence and his failure to resolve this crisis. He knew his father prayed for the success of his precious Sushima at the cost of his other sons. But, Bindusara harboured hatred for Ashoka and wished for the failure of his third son. On the other hand, Ashoka had always believed that he could defy his father's plans with his capabilities and his men by his side.

But now, he felt an odd helplessness in the face of the feeling that destiny had set him up to fail. His anger knew no bounds at this feeling of helplessness and he marched into the prison resolutely.

Dharmasena had been unable to beat out any words from the bound man let alone the truth. Ashoka ordered the man to be unbound. Dharmasena hesitated to comply with the order.

"Udayaditya never hesitates when I order him to do anything. It is a pity that I sent him out of the city to scout for enemies after you expressed suspicions about Deimachus's intentions," Ashoka remarked. "He never questions my orders. He did not say a word in Vidisha and Vaishali."

Dharmasena was hurt. He opened the bounds of the suspected assailant who slumped down weakly on the floor. A moment of respite flooded the man's body as the barrage of blows ended.

But, his respite was short-lived. Ashoka had other plans for the man in mind.

The prince gently took the man's hand in his royal hand and caressed it. Ashoka revealed a strange-looking instrument and clamped its mouth gently on the little finger of the left hand of the suspect. The suspect attempted to catch sight of the prince by opening his swollen eyelid. As he tried to steady his ragged breath, a seething pain suddenly shot through the tip of his little finger in his left hand. The pain spread throughout his body like wildfire and escaped through a scream from his mouth.

His eyelids burst open and his vision cleared. He saw Ashoka hold up the nail he had torn out of his little finger that was bleeding profusely.

"So you do have a voice," Ashoka remarked sardonically. "That means we will get somewhere. Why did you attack the Buddhist nun?"

The suspect pursed his lips shut and breathed heavily to get the pain under control. However, Ashoka's interrogation had just started. Before the suspect could recover, another nail was torn out of the ring finger of the suspect's left hand and another scream escaped his lips.

The people outside recoiled in revulsion at the blood-curdling cries of man. Dharmasena did not flinch, but as the blood seeped out of the wounded fingers, he fought to remain in control.

"This instrument here is called the Simhamukha Yantra. It is an interesting little surgical instrument that was invented by Lord Susruta and its details are given in the Susruta Samhita. I will not bore you with its medical function. But, you can feel its other uses. I need an answer. You have eight fingernails left on your hands and then more on your legs. If that doesn't work, I shall start plucking out your fingers and toes. Fortunately for me, the Almighty has given you a full set. Unfortunately, he has not given you time," Ashoka stated coolly.

He delicately held the hand of the man and immediately pulled out the middle finger's nail on the left hand as the suspect fought to withdraw from Ashoka and stifle a scream. He was unsuccessful on both counts.

"Please," he screamed. 'No more. I was not there to attack her."

Ashoka shook his head sadly. He reached out to pluck another nail out, but the man hastily reaffirmed what he had said earlier and added more details.

"I was there to protect her from another assassin. I work for Lord Somadeva and he ordered me to protect the Buddhist woman," the suspect whimpered. "Please, no more."

Ashoka pulled out another nail and the weak man fought hard to free his hand from the prince's grasp. The man's screams reverberated across the prison.

"Please…no more," the man thrashed around in pain. The persons outside the prison tried to block out the screams and the commander inside tried hard to fight the urge to pry Ashoka away from the suspect.

However, Ashoka remained unfazed and reached out for another nail.

"I told you the truth. What more do you want from me," the suspect frantically shouted in pain.

"What you spun was a web of lies based on the testimony of your victim sitting outside. You must be very intelligent to have your mind working through the torture and spin a story based on the information the woman gave me. Her voice was audible here, was it not."

"That was the truth," the man whimpered, horrified at the thought of Ashoka proceeding to the next nail.

"I do not believe you," Ashoka whispered gently. "I am certain you understand it gives me no pleasure in doing this."

Ashoka reached out to the next nail on the man's left hand to pull it out.

"If I was the attacker, why would I scream and warn the woman? I was sent by Lord Somadeva to protect her. The man was masked in the crowd. He was tall and slim. I saw him moving towards her. I was warning her to move away," the suspect whimpered.

Ashoka brushed away the statement and clamped the pliers-like instrument on the nail of the suspect. However, Dharmasena was quick to stop the prince this time.

"My Prince, please, give him a chance. He seems to be telling the truth. His statement makes sense. Which assassin will scream in a crowd full of people and warn his victim?"

The man whimpered his assent to Dharmasena. Nonetheless, Ashoka pulled out the nail from the man's pointer finger. Another scream and this Dharmasena took a step back.

Ashoka gazed upon his commander who was a man who cut down enemies at one command of his prince. In turn, Dharmasena saw the man who had openly ordered the massacre of the entire banditry of bandits in the forests of Vidisha. Blood had soaked the earth of the forest floor that day and bodies lay strewn in front of Ashoka's Mauryan soldiers. The heads of the bandits were mounted on spikes and placed outside the fort walls of the city as a deterrent against any more illegal activities that meant the harassment of the merchants and the citizens. The locals of Vidisha had themselves been revulsed at the sight, but it served its purpose. The bandits were gone and the merchants were free to travel with their caravans in the forests without any fear. Dharamsena believed in the cause of the prince who wanted to purge the Mauryan empire of everything he deemed unworthy. However, the massacre in the forests of Vidisha was not the full extent of violence of which Ashoka was capable. There was a far darker secret behind the atrocities committed by Ashoka in the Vaishali. Dharamsena brushed away those images from his head and focused on the suspect's testimony. He finally believed that the man was telling the truth.

"So, you are saying that Somadeva hired you to protect his former wife."

The man nodded in acceptance.

"Okay. I need to confirm this statement of yours. Until then, you will be a prisoner," Ashoka said nonchalantly.

As Ashoka walked outside, Dharmasena saw life return into his prince's eyes. Ashoka was himself again.

"Acharyani, forgive me if I have caused you any trouble or inconvenience. You shall be under my protection from now onwards. If what that suspect says is true, your life is still in danger. I promise that I shall protect you and shall ensure that if Somadeva is innocent, no harm shall come upon him too."

Gautami smiled and left with Haridasa. After the two had left, Dharmasena had the suspect securely locked up and accompanied Ashoka outside where the afternoon Sun shone brightly and beat down on their faces. The next few words from Ashoka's mouth convinced Dharmasena that a thousand suns could not conquer the darkness in the prince's heart.

"Dharmasena, all the people who stand in my way and are against me shall be vanquished one day. Never disrespect me in front of strangers like that ever again. When I sit on the throne, I will need loyal commanders. You can be one of them. However, if you are not on my side, then you are against me. It is up to you now to make the decision. Loyalty and obedience are the only two ways to ensure that Acharya Chanakya's vision of Akhanda Bharat can be spread throughout the world. What you did today should never happen again," Ashoka warned his commander.

CHAPTER NINE

PLANS OF CONQUEST

The army moved slowly and carefully through the narrow pass with craggy rocks and boulders surrounding them. Several mountains loomed ahead and a torrential river snaked through large drainage basins carrying copious amounts of water and sediment. A thin layer of ashen-coloured snow carpeted the stunning landscape.

The valley was deep and a fall from the treacherous cliffs above would mean certain death. Had it not been for the flowing water and the occasional echoes of spectral calls, an omnipresent silence would have filled the valley. Nobody seemed in a hurry to exchange any words among themselves. The orders were already conveyed to the soldiers by the captains before the army entered the pass. All the soldiers did now was follow the orders.

Nikaias's gaze was fixed ahead, captivated by the mesmerizing scenery of the landscape. A deputy made a move towards the Mauryan officer and tried to pry information from him.

"So, Mauryan, you have not revealed your name, nor the place where you belong. At least tell me why you hate the

Mauryan Empire. Going by your attire, your turban and the reverence your men hold for you, you must be a captain in the Mauryan Army at least," the Bactrian deputy asked inquisitively.

"I would rather have you concentrate on successfully crossing this treacherous pass. I do not need to answer your questions."

The scathing remark from the Mauryan officer stung the Bactrian deputy into silence.

Nikasias paid no attention to the exchange. He was travelling to Gandhara after years, but this time, he was not a part of a friendly force, but at the helm of a hostile army.

After hours of trepidation and arduous marching, the Bactrian force successfully reached a spot where the mountain corridor widened and revealed a place where they could set up camp. The warriors comprising the ranks of the army were acclimated to the stinging cold of the Himalayas, but the Mauryan soldiers who hailed from the warmer plains of the Ganga river had not been able to bear the biting cold of the mountains despite the layers of animal skins they wore to keep themselves warm. But, their leader paid no heed to their chattering complaints. All he had done was make haste to Bactria to check up on the status of the Bactrian invaders.

As the soldiers went about making camp, the Mauryan made his way to Nikaias's tent, which was large, but shabbily erected due to the haste of the Bactrians to erect their tents for warmth and a little comfort.

The Mauryan asked: "What is the next course of action?"

"We have the element of surprise. We have the superior numbers. And we have the advantage of traitors among the enemy's midst."

"Do not underestimate Prince Ashoka."

"I am not underestimating him. We need to be swift and decisive in destroying the Mauryan army camping at Gandhara. Once we land, we need to send information immediately to your master. He will have Ashoka expelled from Takshasila using his men. Once that is done, the Prince will have no support from Takshasila. We can rout him on the battlefield and hopefully kill him on the field."

"We need to have either Ashoka killed or taken prisoner to break the spirit of the Mauryan Army. Hopefully killed."

Nikaias raised an eyebrow.

"You do not like the Prince very much?"

"I detest all the Mauryans. But, we are not discussing that now," the Muaryan replied dismissively.

"We have to conquer Gandhara before reinforcements from Pataliputra arrive or Antiochus realizes our intentions," Nikaias stated.

"Reinforcements from Pataliputra will not appear any time soon. The Mauryan Emperor hates Ashoka. He wants Ashoka's power base destroyed and will mobilise his forces under Crown Prince Sushima only when he receives word of Ashoka's failure. Emperor Antiochus is still busy in the west of his massive Empire, raising and marshalling troops to fight Emperor Ptolemy of Egypt. This will give you the required time to conquer Gandhara. Also, my patron will take measures to stall Sushima in Pataliputra. The moment is ripe for taking Gandhara," the Mauryan responded.

"You are right. But, now that you think about it, if the Macedonian Ambassador catches wind of our plans, he may try to foil it," Nikaias said, playing the devil's advocate.

"But you said that he may not react and will merely stand by as a spectator." the Mauryan asked incredulously.

"Yes, he will willingly stand by only if he believes that we are making this conquest on behalf of Emperor Antiochus's Empire. That would enable Antiochus to reclaim the lands his father lost to the first Mauryan Emperor. Antiochus would be in a position to use the wealth of Gandhara to pay his armies and he would also be able to bolster his armies with levies from Gandhara," Nikaias said nonchalantly.

"So then make him believe," the Mauryan remarked with exasperation. "My appearance by your side will confuse the Mauryan Army and cause disarray within its ranks. Use that opportunity to break its cohesion and rout it in battle."

"You are a Mauryan yourself. Why do you hate the Mauryans so much?"

"None of your business. I want them gone from Bharatvarsha and the conquest of Gandhara will be the first to cause a chain reaction that will inevitably doom the Empire. So, I request you to kindly march your soldiers into Gandhara in the next two days."

A grin spread on Nikaias's face.

"I will get it done. But your master better get things done in Takshasila. The moment your Prince gets word of the army marching into Gandhara, he will put up stiff resistance. Time is of the essence here and there."

"I do not have a master. The big man in Takshasila is merely my patron. We have an arrangement where the goal is to destroy the Mauryan Empire. Once that is done, we will be going our separate ways. So, you fulfil your end of the bargain and we will fulfil our end of the bargain. Gandhara is large and wealthy enough to fulfil all your wants. You could be the king of a new Indo-Bactrian kingdom."

After having made his pitch, the Mauryan left the tent. Nikaias shrugged and called for the sentinel stationed outside his tent.

"Ask the captains and the men to stay alert. There may be bandits and robbers in every hidden nook and corner of this cloistered mountain passageway. Any news of our man who was sent to look out for the bandits?"

"No, My Lord. We have not received news from him."

"Sending him was a mistake. I should have known his boasts were nothing but hollow words. He better come back with an assurance of safe passage from the bandit chief."

The sentinel seemed uncertain with something which did not escape Nikaias's notice.

"What happened? Speak freely. Out with it."

"My Lord, our soldiers are apprehensive about the barbarians who form a significant portion of our ranks. They feel they are not trustworthy," the sentinel asked apprehensively.

"I do not want to hear any more about this. These so-called barbarians provide us with mobility and enhance our long-range offensive capabilities. Do not spread suspicions about their loyalty to the camp. We need cohesion among our ranks. Now get lost and ask the men to stay alert against any bandits."

The sentinel hurriedly left the tent and Nikaias was left alone with his thoughts. Gandhara was only the beginning. If he pulled off the conquest of Gandhara, he would be in a position to achieve all that the great Alexander could not achieve in his lifetime. The conquest of India.

CHAPTER TEN

The Ambassador visits Samudra

Takshasila suddenly appeared to be alien to me. I received disturbing news from Akshaya about the happenings in the city. Prince Ashoka's arrival in the city should have brought some semblance of normalcy in the city. Instead, it seemed to have thrown the city into turmoil. Trade was reduced to a trickle as entry into and exit from the city was aggressively controlled. Ashoka ignored the protests of the merchants and threatened them with dire consequences if they did not cooperate with him. The city was also forced to feed his army that camped outside the city for the Mauryan prince had brought minimal supplies to ensure he made the march to Takshasila from Pataliputra in the least amount of time possible.

Haridasa too had shared disturbing news about a perceived attack on his friend, Acharyani Gautami. While Varaprada had insisted he keep his voice low, my apprehensive guardian kept his voice shrill due to nervousness about the state of Takshasila's security. Varaprada had a hard time keeping him calm so his words did not reach me. She did not want me to remember the attack that had taken place on me a few days ago. But his words did reach me and a wave of disturbing memories flooded my head.

Prince Ashoka had ordered the Takshasila garrison of Mauryan soldiers to be on the lookout for an assassin who was after Acharyani Gautami's life. This caused Mauryan soldiers to swarm the streets of our neighbourhood because Haridasa had brought his friend to live with us for her security despite her vehement protests.

Now as I sat in my room wondering what could go wrong in the city, we received a visit from four strangers. Three Macedonian soldiers, armoured in a breastplate and equipped with a straight-bladed sword that was scabbarded, swaggered into Haridasa's house followed by a man dressed in a linen tunic and a broad-brimmed kausia hat adorned with two feathers on his head.

As I stared unabashedly at the visitors, the man in the fine tunic bowed a bit and said: "Hello, I am Ambassador Deimachus from Plataea in Greece. I wish to meet the person named Samudra," he said gently in fluent Greek.

In the four years I had lived in Gandhara, one of the languages taught to me was Greek. I could converse in a foreign tongue, though I was not fluent. However, Akshaya was proficient in it. Further, I had seen Greeks in the city and Haridasa was friendly with them, but none of them appeared at our doorstep with armed escorts or bodyguards.

"I am Samudra," I stammered in inarticulate Greek.

"Brilliant," the Greek remarked excitedly, sizing me up from all angles. "I should have guessed it was you. You look different."

Haridasa appeared before the Greek and immediately welcomed him in.

"Lord Deimachus, why do you stand at our doorstep? Please come in.

I wanted to tell him that the four Greek men were already inside our house, but the moment I heard the name of the Greek ambassador, my heart missed a beat.

Deimachus grinned and took a seat, while his guards stood standing guard near the doorway.

"Pandit Haridasa has told me many things about you," Deimachus spoke to me in Prakrit.

I marvelled at the erudition of the man.

Varaprada was quick to serve some delicacies and refreshments and took a seat beside Haridasa. She could see my excitement and smiled gently.

"Lord Deimachus, is it true you have visited Alexandria," I immediately asked him.

Deimachus was taken aback by my excitement.

"Yes, I have been to Alexandria. Beautiful place. It is certainly the jewel of the Mediterranean Sea," he remarked cheerfully.

"Is it true that the world's largest library is located in the city?"

"I do not know if it is the world's largest library, but I do know much of the world's knowledge is stored in that library. It is a truly spectacular repository of human scholarship."

This dramatically increased my excitement and the yearning within me to visit the place.

"Would you take me there, My Lord? I believe it may be hard for a Greek diplomat of Emperor Antiochus's Empire to visit Emperor Ptolemy's Egypt, but if it is within your power, I would like to visit this jewel of the Mediterranean Sea."

Deimachus was left speechless while Haridasa and Varaprada were left gawking at my frankness. But, I was thoroughly taken in by the idea of Alexandria. Alexandria was all I thought about while chaos reigned around me in Takshasila.

"Your enthusiasm is contagious, Samudra, but Alexandria lies in dangerous waters. Emperor Ptolemy may not harm an ambassador. But, he may not allow the entry of Emperor Antiochus's representative into his lands."

"Yes, that is true...but...."

"Enough talking about Alexandria, Samudra," Haridasa interjected. "Let Lord Deimachus state the purpose of his visit."

This intervention from my guardian cooled my enthusiasm.

"It is completely fine. I wanted to see the boy from across the seas. When you mentioned how he arrived in India, I was enthusiastic to meet him."

I grew embarrassed at the attention showered upon me.

"Do you remember anything about the land you originally hailed from?"

"I was a malnourished child when I was found on the shores of Kalinga by the Buddhist monks, Abhaya and Vara. They brought me up under the watchful eye of Abbot Buddhamitra who finally brought me here to Takshasila for my higher studies when I was fourteen years old. He left me in the care of his dear friend, Acharya Haridasa. And since then, Takshasila has been my home."

"Oh. I too am an orphan. I never knew who my parents were but I was taken in by a kind couple who were wealthy in Plataea. My adoptive father was a great orator and statesman. He eventually left his fortunes and lands behind and followed Emperor Alexander O Megas on his grand conquest of the Known World. But, Alexander died young and my father found himself in the service of General Seleucus. Eventually, I found myself in the service of Emperor Antiochus."

"Emperor Antiochus has a keen eye for talent. I have heard of several eminent scholars who are in his service."

I noticed a hint of flattery in Haridasa's words. While Haridasa was quick to praise people, it was rare for him to flatter them. In my opinion, Haridasa was an honest man who conveyed honest emotions. So if Haridasa had resorted to flattering the foreigner, it must have been for a reason.

"Lord Haridasa, you are too kind. I have heard great things about you too."

Both the men laughed heartily, basking in the praise they had heaped upon one another. Suddenly, their laughter evaporated as instantaneously as it had begun. Their faces turned dead serious and an eerie silence descended upon the room.

"What do you think about Prince Ashoka, Lord Haridasa," Deimachus asked the pandit.

Haridasa gave the question some thought and answered carefully.

"Prince Ashoka is an intelligent and capable prince. He has all the makings of a great future ruler."

I, once again, noticed the hint of flattery in Haridasa's voice. He was not being honest. I caught Varaprada eying me. She was signalling me to leave with her. But, curiosity got the better of me and I wanted to see what happened next.

"That was a good answer, Lord Haridasa. How about you tell me what you really think about Prince Ashoka," the Macedonian reiterated his question.

Haridasa turned to face Varaprada and me. He seemed to convey that his answer would take us to a point of no return.

"Prince Ashoka is a powerful man and he is popular among the masses. But he has the makings of a despot. If he ascends the throne, he will be a tyrant who will oppress the people."

A light smile played on Deimachus's lips. But we were not amused.

"So, you seemed to have hit the bull's eye. In the name of crushing treason, the prince has resorted to amassing power and establishing his absolute authority in this region. While Prince Ashoka's attempts to bring peace and security back to Gandhara are praiseworthy, he appears to have an autocratic strain in him. If his subordinates attempt to reason with him, he reveals his autocratic side and implies dire consequences for what he perceives as insubordination. There are rumours about his ruthlessness and brutality when it comes to dealing with crime and dissidence. If he were to sit on the Mauryan Throne, this land may see a new age of tyranny and oppression."

Their words of foreboding hung uneasily in the air. If a dystopian future for the land of Bharatvarsha was all they had to discuss, I found nothing wrong with discussing an exciting trip to Alexandria while the good days lasted.

"But, why are you so concerned with our problems, Lord Deimachus," Haridasa asked sceptically. "Platea is safely nestled on the other side of the continent."

Deimachus's grin returned.

"India was on the other side of the continent too for King Alexander. But did not his armies topple the largest empire the world had ever seen to arrive in your lands? Alexander had approximately forty thousand men when he set out from Macedonia. What is to stop Prince Ashoka from treading a similar path of conquest when he becomes Emperor?"

"You seem certain that Prince Ashoka will become the Emperor."

"I do not know about the other princes of the Mauryan Empire, but Prince Ashoka does not believe that he is entitled to the Mauryan Throne and yet he believes he will ascend it one day. If the rumours about the animosity between him and his father are true, the Mauryan Emperor does not view him as his successor and will raise obstacles to his ascension. But, in the few days that I have observed the Prince from afar, he can and will surmount those obstacles. He writes his fate. So, the contest is clearly between the fated son and the favoured son. Who will win?"

"I hope you do not interfere in this contest merely because you do not want to see Prince Ashoka as Emperor," Haridasa stated, raising an eyebrow.

"I fear Prince Ashoka will be unstoppable when he is Emperor. He may be a tyrant who threatens the peace between the Indian and Greek empires."

"Even Emperor Ajatashatru of Magadha appeared unstoppable when he created war machines to conquer Bharatavarsha. However, Lord Buddha did stop him and convert him into a peaceful and responsible Buddhist monarch," I suddenly intervened, exhausted with the talk of doom and gloom.

"But it was Lord Buddha himself who stopped Emperor Ajatashatru. I have heard that Ajatashatru was the king of Magadha. But Ashoka shall rule Bharatvarsha. When Emperor Chandragupta battled Emperor Seleucus in the northwest, he conclusively defeated the Greek emperor because of his powerful army. It is known that the peace treaty sealed between the two monarchs involved the gift of five hundred elephants from the Indians to the Macedonian Greeks, which Seleucus was happy to accept. When I was on my way to the Governor's Palace, I came across the elephant stables of the merchants and Mauryan garrison. I saw at least fifty of those magnificent beasts and that is just in this city. There must be thousands of those animals in Pataliputra at the command of the Mauryan Emperor. Lord Buddha will not take birth again and again," Deimachus countered immediately. "Where will you find such a man who can stop Ashoka at the helm of his enormously powerful army?"

"You talk as if Prince Ashoka is a demon in the guise of a man and Lord Buddha was a deity. Lord Buddha was born an ordinary man like us. It was time and experience that made him the Buddha. Perhaps, it is time and experience that have demonised Prince Ashoka. We do not know the future and we are already judging him. Perhaps, Prince Ashoka may turn out like Emperor Ajatashatru, but there is hope that he will have a change of heart. Emperor Ajatashatru also saved lives. Emperor Ashoka with his power may also be capable of such deeds. Only time will tell and only history can judge him when his time is up."

Deimachus and Haridasa stared at me for a while with cryptic grins adorning their faces. Only time would reveal the meaning behind those grins for me.

CHAPTER ELEVEN

THE SIGNS OF THE INCOMING STORM

The situation reached a breaking point when a Mauryan soldier caught a suspicious person sneaking out of a merchant's mansion a few days after Ambassador Deimachus visited our house.

Soon the aggrieved merchant was at the garrison, reporting the theft of precious jewels and gems from his treasury and called for the harshest of punishment to be meted out on the person he called a thief.

Oddly, nothing was found on the alleged thief's person and the suspect refused to reveal the purpose of his "late-night visit" to the merchant's mansion. After a whole day's torture, the suspect had not revealed anything. That is when Ashoka personally took over the mission to make the suspect talk.

To the horror of the citizens of Takshasila, the suspect was publicly tied to a pole in the southern section of the city with the prince brandishing a whip, the likes of which were never seen before. Curiosity got the better of the common people who collected in the southern section to witness what would happen to the suspect. The elite however were missing. I also made my way to the place with Akshaya.

The whip was made of coarse leather and its handle and fall appeared ordinary. However, its cracker had numerous teeth-like spikes adorning its end and I couldn't imagine the pain it would inflict upon the helpless 'thief' who squirmed against his binds, trying to free himself.

"Citizens of Takshasila! When I entered our glorious city, I believed that a treasonous few were out to malign the city in the eyes of the Mauryan Crown and I needed to bring them to justice. But, there is a glaring breakdown of law and order in this city if a man such as him breaks into the house of an esteemed merchant when the city reels under a crisis," Ashoka roared, pointing an accusing finger at the suspect who recoiled.

I had not assumed Prince Ashoka to be a theatrical person. But, the show that he put on for the common population had them enraptured. They hung on every word of his.

"And where is Captain Khara in the city's hour of need? How could he shirk his duties like this," Ashoka growled. "Why is he missing from the city when the Garrison needs him?"

I did not understand where the prince was going with this, but I did understand that he was insinuating something.

"The Prince is playing upon public emotions. He is trying to swing the public opinion in his favour," Akshaya asserted and it immediately struck me that he was right.

I remembered the argument between Abbot Buddhamitra and Haridasa all those years ago. Ironically, Haridasa being a resident of Gandhara had sided with the Mauryans, but today the population of Takshasila sided with the Administrative Council. Prince Ashoka already knew something and he was trying to show that to the common people of the city. But, I could not accept the allegations made against Captain Khara, the man who saved my life.

I was about to unwittingly protest against the allegations against Captain Khara when Akshaya quickly reined me in. He asked me to stay quiet and keep my opinions to myself.

As the suspect awaited the infliction of pain at the hands of the prince, Ashoka had another shock reserved for the crowd of people. His soldiers cut through the crowd to reveal a woman, a child and an aged couple who stood quivering in front of the prince.

Suddenly a scream was heard and the suspect started thrashing against his binds.

"Susheela, why are you here? What is the meaning of this? Your Highness, please let them go."

I realised with increasing horror that it was the family of the bound man who stood in front of him. His wife and child would be forced to witness his horrifying ordeal and his aged parents would experience his in his resounding cries. Suddenly, I could not watch anymore. The bound man was already bloodied, but that whip in Ashoka's hands would skin him alive. It took all of Akshaya's strength to keep me quiet. The people watched in rapt attention and waited for what would happen next.

"We should be grateful to the merchant who you robbed for this. Not only was he alert enough to recognise you under the shroud of darkness, but he also revealed your identity and your family to us. I have nothing against you but for the sake of law and order, I have to make a public example of you," Ashoka declared and raised to make the first strike.

But, the whip never drew blood.

"I am not a thief," the suspect screamed as he tried to free himself from his binds. "I am a messenger. I was merely relaying a message to Lord Subhuthi. I do not know what was in the message, but Lord Subhuthi was in touch with some foreigners on behalf of the Administrative Council. The Council is planning something against the Mauryan Government in Gandhara. That is all I know. Please, believe me. I know nothing more. Keep my family out of this. Please, just punish me. Spare them."

There was stunned silence. The crowd witnessed Ashoka discard the whip and signalled his guards to unbind the man. Once the messenger was free, Ashoka drew him close and whispered some words in his ear that completely dissolved any remaining resolve in the man.

"The merchants of Takshasila belong to no one. They owe their loyalty to no one. It took a few slaps to Lord Subhuthi 's face to reveal everything about you. You were nothing but a disposable pawn to him. I am sparing your life because of the information you gave me."

As two guards led the messenger and his family away, Ashoka walked into the crowd and the people parted much like the Red Sea parted for Moses when he led his people to the Promised Land.

As Ashoka made his way through the crowd for a moment his eyes locked with mine and it seemed the whole world stopped. There was no emotion in those eyes. They were glazed over as if a higher power had possessed him and made him do everything he had done to Susheela and her family. When I blinked, the prince was gone. Instead, Ambassador Deimachus stood in his place, surrounded by his guards, wearing a lopsided grin.

"You need to stay on your guard, Samudra. Things are going to get very rough. There is a terrible storm coming from the west. You better brace yourself."

After saying so, Deimachus too went his way and vanished into the crowd. After some time, the crowd dispersed, but I heard murmurs and whispers that did not bode well for the Administrative Council of Gandhara.

CHAPTER TWELVE

THE CROWN PRINCE

While Ashoka brought the city of Takshasila to heel, Pataliputra was preparing for a grand celebration. The crown prince and heir-apparent, Sushima had aged another year and his sycophants predicted that he would soon ascend the Mauryan throne.

The capital city of the Mauryan Empire came alive with music and dance as the air was filled with the fragrant scent of freshly picked jasmine and marigold flowers adorning the royal palace. The constant hum of the common people filled the air as they made their way to the palace grounds to take part in the festivities. The nobles and the courtiers competed and tried to outdo each other to give the most precious items to the firstborn son of the emperor and curry some favour from him.

A grand pavilion was organised in the centre of the palace grounds, its fine silk canopies capable of sheltering thousands of people. A blend of flutes, drums, the stringed Ravanahatha, and cymbals was played to create beautiful yet powerful melodies which regaled the crowds. Groups of graceful dancers, trained in the classical performing arts enshrined in the ancient Natya and Nrithya traditions of Bharatvarsha, performed to entertain the crowds in various corners of the pavilion. These dancers were clad in vibrant silks and cotton clothes, strutting around like peacocks dancing in the monsoon rains.

Tables heavily laden with delicacies both from the country and from foreign shores included spice-infused rice, varieties of meat, colourful fruits, smoked vegetables and sweet desserts infused with saffron.

As Pataliputra celebrated, Emperor Bindusara oversaw these festivities without any peace of mind. While he desperately wanted to revel in the joy of the occasion, his mind was occupied with the tidings in Takshasila. A rider from Ashoka's camp had delivered the news that the Greek diplomat, Deimachus had landed in Gandhara with two hundred horsemen. Ashoka's forces had swelled to four thousand men and he had entered the city without any incident. Oddly, this was the only news he received from the northwest frontier of the empire. There was no news from the surrounding lands due to the curbing of trade and merchant traffic through the northwestern section of the Uttarapatha under Ashoka's orders.

"Your Majesty, what is wrong," Ajita, the Ajivika advisor of the emperor said, interrupting his thoughts. "This is a happy occasion. The whole world bears witness to the might of the Mauryan Empire and its Emperor. Today, the countless births of Prince Sushima shall bear fruition, as he finally heralds a new age of unprecedented peace and prosperity. Prince Sushima shall preside over the greatest empire of Bharatvarsha."

"I already preside over the greatest empire of Bharatvarsha, Ajita," the emperor groaned. "Sushima is bound to inherit this empire from me one day and consequently rule over the greatest empire of Bharatvarsha. But, I am worried about my boy. He knows nothing about the Empire and there is no dearth of enemies. Everyone wants to see my son fail."

A shadow of a smile crossed Ajita's face.

"Your Majesty, Prince Sushima is going to be a wise and powerful ruler. It is his fate to become the Samrat of this country, just as he was fated to be your son. With his rise, he will influence the fate of countless people."

Bindusara faced Ajita with fury in his eyes. The Ajivika scholar was taken aback by the anger of his master.

"Ajita...these are hollow words. You have not fulfilled a single duty towards me as an advisor. Earlier you were able to keep tabs on Ashoka's movements with the use of your spies. But these days, your intelligence cannot be trusted. I appointed you as the teacher of my son and all you have been teaching him is that he is pre-destined to be the Emperor of Bharatvarsha. On the other hand, Ashoka has tamed the most dangerous parts of the Empire. The people adore him, the army respects him and the courtiers favour him. It is because I am still alive and I am the Emperor that everyone views Sushima with favour. But what happens after I am gone? Do you think Ashoka will watch from the sidelines as Sushima ascends the throne? I do not want to accept this but I have seen Ashoka in action. He possesses the talents of my father and he possesses the ambition to achieve greatness. But, he also possesses something that none of my other children possess. I have seen the lust for blood in the eyes of that son of mine. If he is not dealt with, I shudder to think what will happen to Sushima."

Suddenly there was a royal announcement, heralding the arrival of the Crown Prince, Sushima Maurya. As the people crowded on the palace grounds looked up to get a good look at their crown prince. Sushima appeared with a coterie of his followers and sycophants and stood upon an artificial platform erected near the pavilion. The palace grounds erupted with cheers and wishes for the long life of the prince who waved back at the people. A circle of sentinels stood guard at the base of the platform to keep the people from climbing upon the platform and accosting the prince.

Sushima was the spitting image of Bindusara. He possessed a similar physique to his royal father with broad shoulders and rippling muscles. He was also of similar height with unblemished skin and a radiant smile that immediately captivated a person. His body was adorned with gleaming jewels. The emperor's chest swelled with pride and unconditional love as he witnessed his firstborn basking in the adulation of the people. However, a hint of disgust tinged his joy when he witnessed the followers of the crown prince swarm like parasites around him.

As the people cheered, another figure of eminent presence joined Sushima upon the platform to greet the people. Queen Charumitra, the chief consort of the emperor and his favourite queen, was once an eye-catching beauty. However, time had revealed the inner reservoir of strength in the queen and she carried herself with poise and grace. She was confident and her face beamed with pride as the mother of the firstborn and heir–apparent of the powerful Mauryan empire. Her beautiful ladies-in-waiting paled before her commanding presence.

As Sushima waved to the people, his servants brought two sacks filled with gold and silver coins. The prince plunged his hands into a sack and threw a handful of coins to them.

The crowd went wild at this extravagant display of wealth and reached to catch the raining pieces of gold and silver. Sushima's followers joined in the exercise and before long the palace grounds had become a scene of pandemonium with the common people jumping and fighting each other for the coins. The guards at the base of the platform found it hard to maintain control of the crowd and somebody advised the prince to return to his chambers. A couple of attendants and servants on the ground took on the task of distributing food and clothes to the poor and the needy who had gathered to bless the prince on this special occasion and receive alms. Along with his mother, Sushima returned to his chambers in the palace to find his father along with Ajita waiting for him.

"Welcome my son, may you live long and prosper," Bindusara announced as he hugged the apple of his eye.

"Thank you, Father. You have truly arranged for a spectacular celebration for my birthday," Sushima said, evidently delighted.

"This is nothing, my son. There is an even greater celebration awaiting you at night which will ensure that even the deities above will know that it is the birthday of the Crown Prince of the Mauryan Empire."

Saying so, Bindusara revealed a mighty straight sword with a double-edged blade and a jewel-encrusted hilt and pommel. When Sushima received the sword from his father, he realised the weapon was heavy with extremely sharp edges. The weight of the sword was balanced along its entire body, making it easy to wield. As Sushima toyed with his gift, he swung wildly in the air like a child swinging a stick. Suddenly, Ajita came within his sight and mischief crept upon the prince's mind. He pretended not to notice the advisor and swung the sword intentionally in Ajita's direction. The blade of the sword narrowly missed the advisor's head and Ajita jumped back with the reflexes of a cat. Bindusara and Sushima burst out laughing, much to the embarrassment of the Ajivika practitioner.

"Do not worry, Acharya Ajita, I do not think you are fated to die today," Sushima said in amusement. "You have to see me ascend as the Emperor of Bharatvarsha."

"There are princesses from all over Bharatvarsha coming to your celebration. It will be a grand occasion to find you a suitable match," Empress Charumitra said.

Sushima stopped playing with his sword and dismissed the suggestion of his mother.

"Son, you need a suitable woman who will one day stand by you while you rule Bharatvarsha. A woman who will one day give you your heir and continue the Mauryan line. Kalinga is our closest neighbour. Perhaps a marital alliance with that kingdom will finally bring it into our fold. There will be no need for war to conquer the region."

Bindusara looked at his wife with pride. Her political acumen was as good as his closest advisors.

As they were talking, Mamatya Radhagupta suddenly came in and interrupted their conversation. Bindusara was visibly displeased but allowed the chief advisor to speak.

"Your Majesty, Ambassador Deimachus has left Takshasila and is on his way to Pataliputra. He shall be here in three days."

The emperor needed to figure out what to make of the message. The crisis in Takshasila was far from over and Deimachus possibly knew more about the situation on the ground in Takshasila than the Mauryan Crown.

"Sushima, you will be taking care of Ambassador Deimachus's stay in Pataliputra. Anything he wants, give it to him."

Sushima's scrunched up his face in irritation.

"Father, he is an ambassador. Give this task to one of the courtiers. We have hundreds of advisors who can do the job."

"You need to make alliances, Son. By hosting the diplomat, you are sending a message to Emperor Antiochus that his men are welcome in the Mauryan Empire. When you sit on the throne and wear the crown, you will need all the allies you need. That is politics."

"I concur with His Majesty, Your Highness. Ambassador Deimachus is an important man in the Greek world. Getting on his good side is bound to get you in the good books of Emperor Antiochus."

"I do not need to get on the good side of anybody, Mamatya. It is the other way around. I do not remember you giving me your blessings on my birthday," Sushima growled.

"Forgive me, Your Highness. May you live long and prosper," Radhagupta conceded.

"You would be wise to remember these words and your place when I sit on the throne."

Sushima stormed out of the chamber as Radhagupta bowed apologetically. Queen Charumitra followed him, leaving her husband in the company of his advisors. He caught the emperor glaring at him and sighed.

"I want you to help the Crown Prince in his efforts at hosting the Ambassador, Mamatya and there should not be any mistakes," Bindusara warned his chief advisor.

When the emperor too had left, Ajita walked up to his political nemesis and mocked him with hostility.

"When I am Mamatya, I will make sure to advise Emperor Sushima to give you a nice estate on the outskirts of Pataliputra after your retirement. You will not be forced to serve the Emperor's heir as a glorified host for diplomats."

Radhagupta smiled, his face a mask of serenity.

"Do you know something, Ajita? Sushima was born to an emperor. People will accept him as the Emperor one day. But Ashoka was born to be an emperor. People expect him to become the emperor one day. Sushima may ascend the throne, but Ashoka will rule."

CHAPTER THIRTEEN

THE FALLOUT BETWEEN FRIENDS

When a servant brought news about the events in the southern section of the city, Indrabahu was already chairing an emergency meeting between the merchants and the councillors in the wake of troubles created by Subhuthi. As the merchants voiced their displeasure at the treatment meted out to Subhuthi, Indrabahu tried to maintain the peace. But when the servant came and relayed the news, the merchants were too stunned to react. However, Indrabahu was calm and led them to Vasunaga's mansion to have the situation resolved.

Vasunaga heard their complaints and assured them that he would talk to Prince Ashoka and seek clemency for Subhuthi. Despite the merchants leaving him in peace, Vasunaga perceived their growing restlessness and eroding trust in him.

For some reason, Ashoka did not believe that Somadeva was the sole treasonous element in the council and the guild. When everyone except Indrabahu was gone, Vasunaga revealed his plans for the next course of action which shocked his conspirator.

"We have to flee Takshasila and join the Bactrians. Prince Ashoka will stop at nothing when breaking our control of the city. There is no hope for Subhuti. He may be dead already. That nun named Gautami has Ashoka convinced that Somadeva is not entirely guilty and the Prince is out now to uncover the truth. It will not be long before he knows about the Bactrian army that is on its way to lay siege to Takshasila. We can only hope that he is too late in repelling the attack. Until then, it is best if we flee and join the Bactrians in their assault on the city.

However, Indrabahu did not like the suggestion.

"We will be seen as guilty if we flee now. The citizens will view us as enemies if we go and join the Bactrians. And what makes you think Somadeva will let us in? Our goodwill, our reputations and all the work we have done for Gandhara will be undone. We cannot leave."

"Do not be stupid, Indrabahu. I did not expect this from you," Vasunaga hissed. "If we stay back and contest the Prince's power, he will have us executed. Without our inside man to stop him, he has taken control of the garrison, bureaucracy, warehouses, trading routes and even goods. In this situation, there is nothing we can do. Everything that we did was for Gandhara. But, he will not see it like that. We did all we could within the city. Now we'll take it back from beyond its borders. With the defeat of the Mauryans in Takshasila, a new chapter shall unfold in the history of this land."

Indrabahu remained unconvinced.

"Vasunaga, nothing can be proved against us. It was Somadeva who had the Governor attacked, even though it was to scare him. But, he took the blame for that and will not talk. I am sure you have made sure of that. As for Acharyani Gautami, her testament has not proven anything. For all we know, she is defending Somadeva because she still harbours some residual feelings for him from her days as his wife. As long as Somadeva is never found, we are safe. All we need to do is withstand Prince Ashoka and find a way to negotiate with the Bactrians if they successfully seize the city."

Vasunaga grew increasingly frustrated. His machinations had not borne fruit. After the attack on the governor, he had calculated that Prince Sushima would be sent here to deal with the council. He had been confident that a show of peace and some expensive gifts would buy the crown prince's cooperation and he would placate Emperor Bindusara. When the time came, Sushima would ascend the throne and become a puppet, much like Chanakya had once believed that the trio of Vasunaga, Somadeva and Indrabahu would be the puppets of the Mamatya. But disillusionment had struck both sides. But the Takshasila Merchant Guild had become a force unto its own, partly due to the support of Emperor Chandragupta and partly due to the trio's efforts. And now, Ashoka had taken control of the city and would soon be upon them. The only way to take back the city was a pitched battle against the Prince of the Mauryans, in which the victor would get Takshasila.

Vasunaga ordered his servants to appear before him and quickly ordered them to pack everything they could and prepare the caravan. They would be leaving under the cover of the dark through the northern gate of the city. Indrabahu's protests fell upon deaf ears as the de facto Setti of the merchant guild had made up his mind.

"Vasunaga, you will appear guilty and how will you slip out of the city? The Mauryan guards have been on high alert for days for anyone attempting to flee the city. Trust me, do not make the same mistake as Somadeva did. Do not be reckless."

"You dare lecture me on recklessness and what I should do," Vasunaga hissed, losing his cool. "I thought you would understand, but you too are deluding yourself as Somadeva did. All that idiot did was take the blame for the attack on the Governor and the killing of his imprisoned servant. Somadeva is all talk. Did you think he was capable of all the things he took the blame for? Somadeva is a weak man and has only one weakness. Acharyani Gautami is not the one with residual feelings for Somadeva. It is the other way around. Somadeva loved his wife dearly, but never openly displayed it. When he came to know about the attack on the Governor and my plans for Gandhara, he opposed them. He made his choices and he stood against us. He only complained about the Mauryans but never dared to do anything about it. I had to threaten his wife's life to have him take the blame for everything, and much to my surprise, he did everything I asked him to do. I made him the villain, the scapegoat so that Ashoka could focus his energies on capturing him. Excommunicating Somadeva was my last ditch attempt at distancing him from the guild to make Ashoka and everybody else believe that we had nothing to do with whatever happened in the city against the Mauryan Crown. The Bactrian army belongs to me. I shall save the city. It does not matter what the people of Takshasila think. Once we take back the city from Ashoka, all we need to do is toss them a few coins and they will be back on our side. So prepare to flee the city."

Indrabahu backed away from the man who he had believed was his friend and well-wisher. Instead, a stranger stood before him. In turn, Vasunaga too had received his answer.

"When I am back with my army, I do not care if I find you beside the Prince or in the city's dungeons. I will have you executed," the merchant menacingly promised Indrabahu.

Indrabahu left Vasunaga's mansion and made his way to his mansion where he contemplated his next course of action. He had been a fool his whole life, believing everything Vasunaga had told him, never thinking about anything himself. Ashoka would never believe that Indrabahu had no information about Vasunaga's machinations without any proof to back this fact. He may even be executed as a traitor if the prince willed it. On the other hand, he could not flee the city with Vasunaga and risk ostracisation or worse, death as a victim of Vasunaga's schemes.

Then a plan began to form in his head. If he could provide the prince with a token of goodwill, Ashoka may just spare the chief accountant of the Takshasila Merchant Guild his life.

CHAPTER FOURTEEN

A Fragile Reunion

When Deimachus witnessed the size of the army that had crossed the mountain pass through the Himalayas, he was disappointed.

"You brought only five thousand men, Nikaias. How do you expect to take Gandhara with only five thousand men? Even if you defeat Ashoka's army, the Mauryans will send reinforcements. Bindusara will not sit quietly."

The Bactrian general appeared tense as the ambassador rained down criticism upon him.

"I could only arrange for these many men," Nikaias replied with a generous flourish of his hand in a sweeping gesture at the army.

The Bactrians had finally emerged from the pass the previous day with no indication of the Mauryans any wiser. To Nikaias's surprise, Deimachus had appeared at the newly set up camp at the entrance of the pass a few hours after their landing. He had brought two hundred Macedonian horse riders with him along with some servants and attendants. In his conversation with the Bactrian general, he had provided valuable information about the location of the Mauryan army, the state of the defences of Takshasila, the strength of the city's garrison and the mood of the people to the Mauryan occupation of the city.

"Ashoka is not popular among the merchants. However, his attempts at winning the favour of the common people are going well. They have begun viewing him as the lesser evil compared to the merchants and the Council whom they view as exploitative and hypocritical. At least Ashoka's tyranny is transparent."

"Well, if we manage to capture the city and fortify it to the hilt, we can hold it against the Mauryans when they send reinforcements. Once we receive our reinforcements from Bactria, we can rout the Mauryans on the battlefield. For now, we should move under the cover of the forests and through the river. That way, we can surprise the Mauryans and defeat them without sustaining many casualties."

"Do not be hasty. We need to bolster our numbers for a conclusive victory. We could send emissaries to the cities of Bucephala, Sagala and Alexandria on the Indus River. The monsoon season will soon be upon us. Once the rains lash this part of Gandhara, it will be difficult to cross the overflowing river and conquer the remaining parts of Gandhara. This may turn into a long campaign season. For that, we need to be prepared and draw our supplies from somewhere."

"The monsoons can be advantageous for us. The reason Prince Ashoka and his army marched upon Gandhara so quickly was that they did not have to worry about overflowing rivers in the summer season. If we take the city, the Mauryan reinforcements will find it difficult to cross the rivers and reach Takshasila," Nikaias countered.

"You forget that we are foreigners. Even if we take the city with our army, we will not be able to hold it against the overwhelming numbers the Mauryans throw at us."

"You underestimate a well-entrenched position, Deimachus. Our five thousand will be stationed in a well-fortified area with enough rations to feed us. Once we weather the monsoons, we can deal with the Mauryans."

"You underestimate the Mauryans and the monsoons. Do you know how many men Emperor Alexander brought to India to conquer this huge country," Deimachus said exasperatedly.

"Forty thousand veterans. And he had seven thousand horsemen for good measure. Everybody knows that," Nikaias said defensively.

Deimachus nodded in agreement.

"Did you know that the King of Takshasila gave him five thousand men because of jealousy towards King Porus? Do you know how many men the opposing army contained which fought under King Porus?"

"One lakh soldiers with horses, chariots and elephants," Niakias said, wondering where this discussion was going.

"Those are exaggerated numbers. The accurate numbers were thirty-five thousand men with four thousand horsemen, three hundred chariots and two hundred elephants. The armies were almost equal on both sides."

"Okay, so what are we discussing here," Nikaias snapped irritatedly.

"The two reasons why Emperor Alexander won were because of excellent field tactics and a monsoon that played havoc against Porus's elephants. While the casualties on Porus's side were ten times that of Emperor Alexander, Porus was not the monarch of India. He was merely a king of a tiny fraction of India's northwest border. Dhana Nanda of Magdha was the mightiest king of India then and he awaited with an army five times the size of Alexander's army with a kingdom that was not even half the size of the Persian Empire. We do not know whether Emperor Alexander would be victorious against Dhana Nanda of Magadha, but we certainly do know of how Alexander's successor, Emperor Seleucus fared against Chandragupta Maurya, a monarch far stronger than Dhana Nanda. Arguably, Chandragupta's son commands an even greater empire. We need to unite all the Greek military manpower we can assemble into a strong army. Five thousand fighting men is not enough when an army of sixty thousand marches upon us after the end of monsoon season. If we secure Gandhara with the assistance of the Greeks from Bucephala, Sagala and Alexandria, Emperor Antiochus will take heed of our cause and will help us engage the Mauryans. Victory will be ours."

"We have not prepared for a lengthy monsoon campaign season. We do not have the supplies," Nikaias resisted.

"We will have the supplies along with fighting men from the Greek cities. Trust me. I, myself, shall travel to Bucephala and get support."

Nikaias was not convinced, but his resistance weakened.

"By the way, how did you get past the Prince and reach here?"

"My spies had already informed me that there was a suspicious buildup of military manpower at Bactria's southern border. I anticipated that the Bactrians would use the mountain pass that led into the Indus Valley. All I had to do was kill time until your army reached the valley. However, I did not think I would meet you, but I could approximately estimate the amount of time it would take for your army to reach here. I told Ashoka it was time for me to travel to Pataliputra and he was more than happy to see me go. So, here I am."

"It is fortunate we found an ally in you, Deimachus," a raspy voice interrupted the exchange between the Macedonian and the Bactrian.

Vasunaga hobbled towards them and greeted them with a courteous nod.

"I do not remember you being this courteous to us, Lord Vasunaga," Deimachus remarked, teasing the merchant. "The last time I met you, there was something cold in your demeanour. I thought you had forgotten this friend of yours."

"I was just putting up an act. Also, I was not aware of your intentions. I needed to be careful."

"I hope you have no doubts after I smuggled you out of Takshasila to the relative safety of Nikaias's camp."

Vasunaga gave the diplomat a rare smile.

"You saved my life and my gold. If you had not smuggled me and my aides out, I would either be caught by the Prince or pay hefty bribes to the sentinels of the North Gate to allow me to escape."

"Some influence over those sentinels will always come in handy. When the time comes, our main army can fight Ashoka on the outskirts of the city while a team of elite soldiers infiltrates and takes the city from within."

"I do not need influence for that. All I need is my Mauryan pet," Vasunaga said. "He can simply walk into the city with his men and dispatch with the Prince if needed."

"Now that the three of us have united, we are in a ripe position to take out Prince Ashoka and instal a new power in the region. Deimachus's brains, my brawn and Vasunaga's brine," Nikaias said aggressively.

"Vasunaga's brine?"

"If Takshashila is considered as water, Vasunaga's men are the salt that has completely dissolved in that water. Salt dissolved in water produces brine. When the time comes, your brains and my brawn will take the city from the outside and his brine will give us from the inside."

"Well said, Nikaias. I know Emperor Antiochus needs the support of Gandhara for support from Bactria has proven unreliable. Once we secure this region and finish Ashoka, you could have the Satrapy of Gandhara. Vasunaga could formally have the much-needed autonomy to expand his business, especially that of horses and spices in the Greek lands and I could ascend the ranks to become the right-hand man of Emperor Antiochus. Then we can always turn our attention to Bactria and other regions in India," Deimachus asserted with excitement.

But the contagious excitement did not spread to the merchant.

"Do not count the goose's golden eggs before the goose has laid them. We need to have patience and tread carefully. Ashoka is not one to be taken lightly."

"You are quoting the moral of a popular Aesop's fable to us," Deimachus remarked amusedly. "We shall heed your advice, oh wise one. We should use that Mauryan pet of yours to spread disinformation among Ashoka's army and destroy their unity from within. Then destroying him shall be easy."

"Do you hate Prince Ashoka, Deimachus," Nikaias enquired the ambassador. "You speak about destroying Ashoka personally instead of the Mauryans."

"I have seen the darkness in that man, Nikaias. He is bad news. Alexander considered himself the Son of Zeus, legitimising his ambition and he established the greatest empire in the known world. I have seen that fire in Ashoka's eyes, but his ambition could spell the doom of the Greek empires. His empire may not extend to Macedonia, but if given free rein as the Emperor of India, he could pose a threat to Emperor Antiochus's Greek Empire by allying with Emperor Ptolemy. But then there could be hope…"

Deimachus immediately brushed aside the thoughts in his mind.

"Geopolitics has never been my strong suit. All I want is a kingdom that I can call my own," Nikaias revealed. "I do not mind if it is Gandhara."

Just then, the Mauryan agent of Vasunaga appeared on the scene. Deimacus was shocked to see him.

"Lord Vasunaga, I am pleased to see you hale and hearty," he said with folded hands.

"It is good to see you are safe too," Vasunaga replied.

"I also wanted to apologise for mistreating you earlier, My Lord. I hope you understand it was a part of my act."

"I understood. It was very convincing."

The agent bowed and left. Vasunaga turned to find Deimachus at a loss for words. He was proud that the revelation of his agent had left the diplomat dumbfounded.

"I found him at a slave bazaar. He was a malnourished, dirty and quiet youth. But then, I found something else in his eyes. I saw defiance and hatred in them. When I bought him, two Mauryan guards crossed our path. The youth's throat was parched but he took the time to spit at them."

Vasunaga let out a guttural guffaw that took the Greek and Bactrian by surprise.

"The soldiers immediately started beating him up and I had to apologise profusely on his behalf. But that day I came to know that his hatred for the Mauryans was boundless. It turned out that he was also very strong and had a talent for learning quickly. I ensured he was well-fed, his hatred was nurtured and then sent him on his way to join the Mauryan army."

"You thought you could destroy the army from the inside," Nikaias interjected.

"Yes. The Mauryans are too powerful to be challenged from the outside. So, I sent people to infiltrate their organisations and destroy them from the inside. I honed the skills of another youth named Ajita, an Ajivika scholar, but he betrayed me. However, I do not need him anymore. He has served his purpose."

"And what purpose is that," Deimachus asked.

Vasunaga hesitated. If he answered this question, he would cross the line of no return.

"Did you know it was indirectly due to Chanakya that Bindusara lost his mother and got his unfortunate name?"

"Yes, the whole of India knows that tale. It was unfortunate that Queen Durdhara was poisoned accidentally while eating the Emperor's food laced with poison. I believe it was to increase his tolerance to poison."

"Exactly. This caused Bindusara to hate Chanakya when he was made aware of this open secret in his youth. When he became Emperor, he ousted Chanakya from his court and sent him to live on the outskirts of Pataliputra. Chanakya's involuntary retirement caused a massive power vacuum which Radhagupta and Ajita filled. I sent Ajita to the Mauryan Court and he was an instant hit. His success was far beyond my wildest dreams. Ajita had been sent there to poison Bindusara against his father's advisors and ensure that the Emperor intervened as minimally as possible in Gandhara's affairs. That coupled with a weak Governor ensured that the Administrative Council was in charge of Gandhara's affairs. Meanwhile, the young Crown Prince was handed over to Ajita to be moulded into the future emperor. That is when Chanakya threatened us again. He began meddling in our affairs again and even the ire of the Emperor did not dissuade him. So, I told Ajita to have Bindusara deal with him. But Ajita took an alternate meaning to my orders."

Deimachus's eyes widened in shock

"How did a merchant from the farthest corner of the Empire kill the architect of the Mauryan Empire?"

"By weaponising the hatred of an emperor and lots of luck. Ajita found a low-level, but ambitious minister named Subandhu who was willing to go to any length to become one of the high-ranking advisors of the Emperor. Ajita convinced him that the Emperor wanted Chanakya dead, but it should not be traced back to him. Anyone who achieved that task would be made a principal advisor.

Subandhu, a blind idiot, hired men who set fire to Chanakya's hut one night and the once great Mamatya of Chandragupta Maurya burned along with it. I cannot confirm it, but the two of the hired men charged into the hut without thinking to kill him and they set off a contraption which released a poisonous perfume which caused their skin to erupt in painful blisters and their eventual deaths. Crafty old fox was prepared to take anyone who tried to kill him with him to death. Witnesses said that Chanakya's spirit had cursed the perpetrators of his death."

Nikaias shrugged his shoulders, but Deimachus could not digest the information shared with him.

"When news about Chanakya's death spread, the public outrage was immense. Rumours abounded that Bindusara had the Mamatya killed because nobody else in the Empire had the courage and power to kill Chanakya himself. The crooked Brahmana had everybody convinced that he could perform magical feats. From when he created gold to support Chandragupta's war campaign against the Nandas of Magadha to when he mysteriously orchestrated the deaths of all of the political rivals of his protege to ensure his ascendancy and eventual victory. I believe he concocted the story that Chandragupta belonged to the royal lineage of the Ganasangha of Pipphalivana. Nobody could confirm his words and when Chandragupta saved the people from the tyranny of Dhana Nanda, he created the persona that Chandragupta was a saviour, an avenger who had completed his vengeance against the oppressive Nandas who had wiped away the Moriya Republic during Dhana Nanda's empire building activities. He even had Jhadamitra, the Setti of the Takshasila Merchant Guild killed to protect his secrets and reputation. He attempted to use such a brutal crime to curb the growing influence of the merchants in northern Bharatvarsha but failed to do so. We were fortunate that Chandragupta could think for himself instead of being swept away in the lies Chanakya fed him. Bindusara was suspicious, but he was stupid enough to believe the words fed by sycophants and false well-wishers. But, Ashoka neither possesses Chandragupta's common sense nor does he keep the company of sycophants. He will listen to no one other than himself and do as he pleases."

Nikaias was done listening to the tale. He rose to his full height and screamed at the top of his lungs.

"Soldiers, prepare to march. We need to reach Takshasila as soon as possible. So prepare to march, now."

As his orders spread like a wave among his soldiers, Deimachus approached the merchant.

"Vasunaga, I suggest you stay back with the reserves at the place where we set up camp. And send your agent to Takhshasila now. But, do not send him empty-handed. Give a gift to Ashoka that gives him a false sense of hope. I hope you understand what I mean."

"You are really generous, Deimachus."

"No need to be sarcastic. Also, if anything were to happen to us, you should prepare to flee. If we win, we shall send you word of our victory. "

"I am amazed, Deimachus. You value my life over yours," Vasunaga said sceptically.

"It is not like that old friend. From your tale, it appears that fortune has favoured you so far. But, things change. Once Ashoka knows what I have done, he will come for my head. But, I believe if he captures you, you will suffer a fate far worse than death."

CHAPTER FIFTEEN

KHARA RETURNS

When Ashoka stood in the Governor's Palace overlooking the great city that stood as the jewel of the Mauryan empire's northwest border, frustration was all that filled his heart.

Everything was too quiet. There was sporadic unrest and resistance to his new policies, but he quickly arrested the troublemakers and imprisoned them. Udayaditya was yet to arrive with any credible information on whether there was any suspicious military build-up along the neighbouring Greek empire or its Bactrian outpost. But, Deimachus knew something suspicious was going on in Gandhara and may have contacted his overlord. Ashoka had tried to prevent any leaks in intelligence by sealing the borders and screening everything coming into and going out of Takshasila, but Deimachus was a crafty fox. He may have found a way to smuggle information to Antiochus, which meant that Ashoka needed Udayaditya's verification of Dharmasena's suspicions more than ever. Fortunately, Deimachus had left for Pataliputra and Ashoka had made sure that the Greek diplomat was nowhere near the great Western Greek empire.

But, his real troubles lay with the fact that Vasunaga, the de facto Setti of the Takshasila Merchant Guild and the power behind the Administrative Council had slipped right under his nose and fled the city. Subhuthi had sung like a bird at the mention of torture, but he did not reveal anything that linked Vasunaga to the assassination attempt on the Governor and the murder of the suspect. However, Subhuthi did reveal that Vasunaga was behind the manipulation of the Mauryan governor of Gandhara who heaped unwarranted benefits and concessions upon the merchants. With his testimony, Ashoka was confident that he could arrest the merchant prince without any questions. But the merchant had slipped past the sealed gates and escaped from the city.

Ashoka had ordered the guards positioned on the four gates flogged outside the city and to have them executed so that the other Mauryan soldiers did not witness the punishment. Dharmasena remembered how Ashoka had stood before Bindusara and proudly explained that diplomatic negotiations were the key to catching the perpetrators behind the treasonous acts against the Mauryan crown in Takshasila and blood would not be shed in the process. But, Ashoka was no different from his father. It was ironic that he was setting an example against treason by shedding the blood of the very people who were meant to check treason. The commander had always believed that the executions in Vidisha and Vriji were needed to suppress the divisive elements that threatened the unity and stability of the empire. But, the execution of twenty Mauryan soldiers would not be tolerated. The city was already rife with rumours that the prince was cruel and unhinged. The citizenry merely sided with him because they viwed the merchants as the reason behind their woes.

The punishment meted out on the twenty soldiers would certainly cause them to openly rebel against him. In his quest to suppress the treasonous elements that threatened the empire, he was busy slaughtering his allies because he suffered from infirmities of the body due to the bad karma from his previous births. When Dharmasena finally gathered his courage to question the prince, the prince silenced him with an answer and sent him on his way.

Either way, Ashoka was unconcerned. He had his men study the entry and exit points in the city to find weaknesses. He suspected that the merchant had bribed his way out of the city and was on his way to Bactria or to Greco-Persia.

As he was calculating his next move, a guard came in and gave him a shocking piece of news.

"Your Highness, Captain Khara has returned with a strange man in tow. He seeks an immediate audience with you. He says it is extremely urgent and is an emergency."

"Let him in at once and make sure you position guards outside this chamber. There will be no mistakes this time," Ashoka thundered.

The guard ran out and ushered in a ragged-looking man and Khara into the chamber. Ashoka noted that Khara had a look of pride and satisfaction on his face, while the man dressed in rags looked broken and defeated.

"Your Highness," Khara said victoriously, "I present to you Lord Somadeva of the Takshasila Merchant Guild."

Ashoka's eyes widened in surprise as the once-arrogant merchant slumped to the ground and bowed in front of the prince.

"I am not worthy of the mercy of the Lord of Gandhara, but in return for the information I provide to you, I implore you to protect Gautami from Vasunaga. I will obey everything you say as long as I know Gautami is safe."

"Who are you to negotiate with me? Who gave you the authority to dictate terms to me," Ashoka fulminated. "Your city stands today because I will it. If I had listened to my father, I would have had it razed to the ground."

Somadeva was terror-struck and immediately recoiled at this verbal attack. He dragged himself away from the prince who menacingly covered the distance and exuded a hostile intent to kill him on the spot. But Ashoka did not act on that impulse. Instead, he turned his ire upon Khara which immediately wiped away the smile of the captain.

"Captain Khara, why did you shirk your duties as a garrison captain and desert your station? Are you working in cahoots with the enemy? Are you a traitor?"

"Your Highness, these allegations are baseless. I did not desert anyone. I had a gut feeling that Acharyani Gautami's words provided a valuable lead to us. But, I decided to keep information within my inner circle of soldiers. I could not risk warning her attackers about what I intended to do. I had to find Somadeva to unearth the conspiracy against the Mauryan Crown in Gandhara. But, I had sent word of my plan to you through my trusted man. He conveyed my plans to your commander because he was not allowed to meet you. It was only then I set out to hunt down Somadeva."

Ashoka was seething from within. Khara's defiance infuriated him.

"I did not receive any such word of your so-called plans. It is convenient for you to claim that to prevent any intelligence leaks you decided to keep your plan within your trusted inner circle. Then you claimed to share this plan with my commander because I was not available."

"You too have closed the gates of Takhsasila to the world, Your Highness for preventing the external enemies of the Mauryan Empire from knowing about the internal troubles of Gandhara. But, you have not shared your reasons with the people because you do not trust them. If you have your reasons to keep secrets, I have mine."

"Guards! Guards!"

At the prince's angry call, Mauryan soldiers poured into the chamber and surrounded Khara. The garrison captain noted the unfamiliar faces surrounding him and understood these were Ashoka's men. He sighed in resignation and surrendered to his fate.

Ashoka ordered Khara and Somadeva to be taken away and imprisoned. As Khara and Somadeva were being led away, the captain found Ashoka eying him curiously. Khara immediately averted his eyes. But Somadeva glared at Ashoka with open hostility.

"You are no ruler of Gandhara. You are just a tyrant. I shudder to think about the future of Bharatvarsha."

Just then another guard appeared and announced another visitor for the prince. Ashoka was irritated.

"Who is this visitor who wants to see me now," he snapped.

"Forgive me, My Prince, it is the merchant known as Indrabahu who wishes to meet you."

Ashoka was suddenly most interested and conveyed the same to the guard.

"Send him in. Quickly send him in. I want to see what the dog has to tell me when his master has fled the Empire."

CHAPTER SIXTEEN

THE PRINCE AND THE MERCHANTS

Akshaya and I were in the northern section of the city when the giant gate in the north opened to allow the entry of a Mauryan squad of soldiers who looked exhausted and weather-beaten. At the helm of the squad was a grave-looking, lean-muscled man who was the commanding officer of the men. I could not get a clear look at his face, but he looked oddly familiar to me and I could not divert my gaze away from him.

However, my gaze was diverted when I saw a couple of ragged-looking foreigners bound to the horses of some Mauryan soldiers and being dragged along the dirt. They were barely conscious and looked like they were in desperate need of food and water.

The crowd quickly parted to let the squad pass and as the Mauryans rode through the way, the commanding officer's eyes met mine. I tried hard to remember where I had seen that face, but somehow, the memory eluded me. Before I could place the memory, the squad was gone, possibly off to the Governor's Palace in the central section.

"What are you thinking, Samudra? Where are you lost," Akshaya asked.

"I feel like I have seen the commanding officer of the Mauryan squad that just passed by. But I do not know where."

"Do not put too much pressure on your mind. That was Commander Udayaditya, an officer from the inner circle of Prince Ashoka. There is no way you would have seen him before in your life unless Prince Ashoka was in Kalinga before coming to Gandhara."

"You have a point."

Akshaya and I made our way to a meeting of merchants where the primary topic of discussion was how to convince Ashoka to spare some trade concessions and lift some of the restrictions upon trade in the city of Takshasila.

"We do not have a say anymore in the matters of governance," one of the merchants snapped. "Prince Ashoka has seized power from the Governor and has installed his men in positions of bureaucracy. Vasunaga has also fled the city. What will happen to us?"

The merchant had merely voiced aloud the doubts and questions that were on everyone's minds.

"Do not fret. The Prince will soon grant us concessions," came a voice which raised the faces of the forlorn merchants.

Indrabahu confidently walked into the midst of the merchants and reiterated his words of assurance to the others present in the meeting.

"I had a one-on-one meeting with Prince Ashoka. I made some demands and accepted some demands. It was a simple transaction. Due to Vasunaga fleeing the city instead of surrendering to the Prince, martial law will be imposed upon the city and the Administrative Council will be dissolved. There is a good chance we are heading towards a war and Vasunaga will join Takshasila's enemies. However, if we do not support Vasunaga, he has assured us that after his victory over the Empire's enemies, the Council will be reconstituted and we will be made a part of the reconstruction efforts with a greater say in governance once peace is established again. All our offences and crimes against the Mauryan Crown will be forgiven."

Murmurs and whispers abounded as there was a clear split on the further course of action. For a few merchants, the idea of a royal pardon and no prosecution after the end of the war seemed attractive enough to command their support. However, others did not trust the Prince to keep his word. Vasunaga may have fled the city, but there was a consensus that he would return to safeguard his commercial interests in the region. He had too much to lose. It was one of these opposing merchants who gave voice to these thoughts.

"What makes you think that Ashoka will keep his word and what makes you think that Vasunaga will take everything lying down? If we support the Prince and the Mauryans lose the war, Vasunaga will not spare us. But, if we do not support Ashoka and pledge our support to Vasunaga and we lose the war, Ashoka will have us executed. Can you give us any assurance that our families and interests will be safeguarded?"

Indrabahu smiled.

"I assure you that Prince Ashoka will not harm us, our interests or our family because we hold something very dear to him. However, we must assure him that we will not side with the merchant, Vasunaga. And when the Prince calls for our help, we must answer his call," Indrabahu specified.

"You still have not answered what happens if Vasunaga wins the battle," the disgruntled opposing merchant asked.

"You better hope that Vasunaga neither wins nor returns, for if he does, every one of you will lose and have your properties confiscated by him when he takes back the Guild irrespective of that person being a traitor or supporter of his cause."

"He cannot do that," the merchant replied defensively. "He needs the members of the Guild to run the assortment of businesses that fall under the purview of the Guild. How will he do it alone?"

"What makes you think he needs Indian merchants to run his Guild's businesses? He consorts with the foreign merchants of Bactria. There is a Bactrian army which has landed on Gandharan soil and it is coming to take our home away. Vasunaga has made his bed with the enemy. Our best option for survival is Prince Ashoka and trust me when I tell you that I have made a deal with the Prince. But we must rally behind that. I have the means to ensure he keeps his word. I cannot tell you what leverage I hold upon him, but I do know that it is powerful enough to ensure that a man like Prince Ashoka too will keep his word. If I were to tell you, we would lose the leverage."

The merchants weighed the assurance of the chief accountant of the guild. Somadeva had created this mess and Vasunaga had abandoned them. Only Indrabahu stood here, assuring them that the guild and their hold over Takshasila would survive. But, they had to work with the Mauryans. They had no other choice. Therefore, they accepted Indrabahu's assurance and decided on the next course of action.

Elsewhere, Ashoka wondered if he had made the right decision by making a deal with Indrabahu. The prince had the army and the prince held the administration of Gandhara in his hands, but Indrabahu still enjoyed the fragile trust of the mercantile class of Gandhara and a secret that could destroy the foundation of the empire.

As he contemplated the options before him, he received news that Udayaditya had finally returned with a few prisoners.

Finally! He is here.

When Ashoka rushed to meet his commander, he was brimming with anticipation. Perhaps, Udayaditya had something that could prevent the jeopardising of his fortunes in Takshasila. Ashoka was not disappointed.

"My Prince, forgive me for the delay, but I have some troubling news. An army of approximately five thousand Bactrians have landed in Gandhara through the mountain pass connecting Bactria with this region. They will be here in two days. Further, one of my men saw Ambassador Deimachus with the Bactrians. The Greeks are not on the road to Pataliputra. They are in northwest Gandhara and have joined hands with the Bactrians to launch an assault on us."

This news hit Ashoka like a jolt of lightning, but he recovered quickly.

"Are you certain Ambassador Deimachus is with the Bactrians? You may have made a mistake. He left Takshasila a few days ago."

Udayaditya signalled a guard to bring in two of the prisoners he had brought with him.

"My Prince, this man is a Bactrian scout who was caught along with three others when they were trying to spy on our army and this man is a Greek soldier belonging to Deimachus's army. I was returning with no information when fortune favoured me by landing these foreign scouts right into my hands. However, I did have a scuffle with a Bactrian cavalry unit while apprehending them. In that scuffle, I lost some men, but I did capture the scouts and managed to give them the slip. The only drawback is that the survivors of that unit will go back and report what we know about their landing and their numerical strength. They may change their attack strategy after their encounter with my men."

Udayaditya slapped the Bactrian scout hard. Ashoka had a person who spoke perfect Bactrian brought into his chambers. When Udayaditya questioned the scout about his army's strength and tactics, the man revealed that the Bactrians were going to attack the Mauryans in an all-out attack on the outskirts of Takshasila to use their superior numbers and the newly formed Greek unit which Deimachus had added to the army. The Bactrians knew that the Mauryans had a smaller army due to information relayed by the Greek ambassador and that there were possible reinforcements expected from Emperor Antiochus in case things went south for the invaders.

Before Udayaditya could question the Greek prisoner to verify the information given by the Bactrian, the bound Greek soldier fell at the feet of the prince, begging for mercy. Ashoka was quick to catch him by the shoulders and roughly hoist him to his feet. In the process of manhandling the scout, Ashoka felt a gentle prick in his hand as he felt the hand of the prisoner brush over his hand. The prince forcefully pushed back the scout and curled his hand into a fist.

Ashoka turned and walked to a corner of the room. Udayaditya could feel the frustration of the prince even with his back turned to his commander. The prince let out a high-pitched roar as he smashed his fist against a wall, drawing blood.

"How could I have been so careless? I should have sent a unit of soldiers to shadow the ambassador and uncover his true motives."

Udayaditya was quick to defend him.

"My Prince, that would not have done us any good. The unit could not have stopped him and would have been intercepted and slaughtered by the Bactrian cavalry. Your army would have suffered early casualties and the Greeks would have blamed you for attacking a friendly force while lying through their teeth about their own motives. We can still win because we know this terrain. With patience and better field tactics, we can overcome their superior numbers."

"No Udayaditya, we do not know the terrain as well as Vasunaga. I am certain that the traitorous merchant has also joined the Bactrians. He will join whatever strength he possesses with the Bactrians and the Greeks. It will seem like a civil war and the population of Gandhara will see me as a tyrant shedding the blood of my own citizens. If I give the Bactrians a pitched battle, they will win using superior numbers. Further, if the Bactrian army hides in the forests surrounding Takshasila, it will be difficult to face them. And, if I allow them to lay siege to the city, there is a good chance that the citizenry of Takshasila will stab me in the back and hand me over to Vasunaga for execution."

Ashoka quickly ordered one of the soldiers to have Dharmasena appear before him. The Mauryan commander was quick to follow the orders and heed the summons of his prince.

"My Prince, you summoned me," he said with folded hands.

"Dharmasena, have my orders been carried out?"

Dharmasena bowed his head and replied.

"The erring sentinels have been executed on the outskirts of Takshasila, as per your orders. However, there were witnesses to the punishment, My Prince."

"What? What happened to those witnesses?"

"They escaped Your Highness. They ran into the wilderness that borders Takshasila."

"Fine, I do not have the time to deal with them. Let the wilderness claim them. Udayaditya, you have travelled the terrain from here to the north. How many days do you think the foreign army will take to reach the city?"

"Your Highness, the Bactrian army will be here in approximately two days. It will take them longer if they decide to march to Mansehra and recover there."

"That hardly leaves us with any time. Dharmasena and Udayaditya, prepare the army. We shall march at night."

"My Prince, the soldiers will not be ready by then. Also, we must leave a defence force behind to protect the city, in case the Bactrian army lays siege to the city."

"Muster as many soldiers as possible. I want an army prepared to march by nightfall. The Bactrian cavalry is certainly part of a larger force that is marching upon us. We need to ensure that we meet them on the open battlefield. Also, I believe it is going to rain finally today."

But what about the superior numbers of the Bactrians? Also, is it wise to lead the men during the onslaught of the rains?

Ashoka read the thoughts of his commander and sighed.

"I need an army prepared to march before the other soldiers know that there are twenty missing soldiers. Also, I have a surprise for our Bactrian friends when the time comes."

Udayaditya cast a glance at Dharmasena and the other commander met his gesture.

"Twenty missing soldiers," Udayaditya's gesture conveyed a question.

"Twenty executed soldiers," Dharmasena's gesture conveyed the answer. "I will explain later."

Udayaditya's face conveyed no surprise, but he conveyed his understanding with a slight nod.

"Udayaditya, I need you to take up the job of defending the city. Other than the two hundred Mauryan guards of the Takshasila Garrison, I will leave behind a unit of Mauryan soldiers to help bolster the city defences. While we leave, I need you to undertake whatever fortifications of the city that you can. I am counting upon you."

For the first time since he appeared before Ashoka, Udayaditya's face registered shock.

"My Prince, I am not a city defender. I am the commander of your army's left flank. Permit me to accompany you to the battlefield so that I can fight by your side."

Ashoka placed a hand on his trusted commander's shoulder and justified his order.

"Udaya, I need you here. I cannot trust my own soldiers," Ashoka's voice reduced to a whisper.

"I just had Captain Khara of the Takshasila Garrison arrested for desertion. For some reason, he was accompanied by the elusive traitor, Somadeva, the ex-councillor of the Administrative Council. He claimed that he had left the defence of the city to trusted men to capture Somadeva. He also made an absurd claim that he had relayed information about his plans to my commander. Dharmasena did not share anything with me. Did any man from Somadeva come to you with any information about his plans?"

Udaya's impassive eyes widened in surprise.

"No, Your Highness. I have had no contact with Captain Khara or his man about his plans. I immediately left the city to scout certain areas in Gandhara to check if any potential enemies of the Empire lurked on the fringes. Turns out, Dharmasena's suspicions and your instincts were right. Some enemies are making their way to the city as we speak."

Ashoka smiled comfortingly.

"That is what I wanted to hear, Udaya. It is for that reason that I am leaving you in charge of the city. Perhaps, Khara had been turned by the merchants to their side, or he had always been on their payroll. Either way, if the Mauryan guards in the city come to know that I have imprisoned him, they may turn against us. I need you as my voice here to keep them in check. When I return, I shall punish Khara and make an example out of him. Until then, he is not to be touched. I do not want a rebellion on our hands. But, Somadeva is to be questioned. I leave you in charge of that. Find out whatever you can. Do whatever you have to. I want to know everything Somadeva knows about Vasunaga and his plans. Meanwhile, I will find a suitable commander for my left flank. I want the questioning to begin as soon as I leave."

After having issued the orders Ashoka dismissed the officers.

As Dharmasena and Udayaditya left the chamber, Udayaditya comforted Dharmasena, much to the latter's surprise.

"Everything will be fine. The city will be safe and the Maurryan soldiers here will be well. Just focus on the battle."

Dharmasena was taken aback. Udayaditya was not one to display such warmth. The man was a quiet soldier who operated with stone-cold efficiency. In the years that the two commanders had interacted with each other, Udayaditya had merely acknowledged Dharmasena's words with a gruff grunt or sharp nod. Dharmasena was quick to realise that Udaya's non-verbal reactions were the only reaction he would get. The man only opened his mouth to issue orders to his subordinates or relay reports to his counterparts and the prince. Udaya always controlled his emotions and kept his thoughts to himself. Further, Udaya had never comforted Dharmasena before.

I guess there is a first time for everything.

Dharmasena gratefully acknowledged Udaya's comforting words and marched to order the captains to prepare the army to march by nightfall.

The moment Dharmasena was out of sight, Udaya's softness vanished and his impassivity returned. He made his way to his trusted men and issued the prince's orders to them.

"I want the walls manned in four shifts. All the watchtowers need to be occupied by our soldiers. Check the walls for any weak points and plug them in. One of you checks the food reserves of the city. If the enemy successfully lays siege to the city, we need to thwart their assault on our walls. Just before our arrival, the traitor Somadeva was arrested by the Prince. Get some food into his belly. I suspect he will not be eating for a long time."

Udaya's men immediately scattered to fulfil his orders. Meanwhile, Dharmasena issued orders to the captains of the Mauryan army to gather their men and prepare them to march.

As Ashoka supervised the preparations of the army, he decided to leave behind five hundred men in the city while marching out with a three thousand five hundred strong army of veterans and inexperienced soldiers alike.

As the preparations were completed and the shroud of darkness fell upon the city, all the classes from scholars, merchants and the common people witnessed Ashoka dressed in his regal armour with his commander, Dharmasena by his side, lead their army out of the city through the northern gate. Ashoka had insisted that Udaya look into the fortifications of the city and not waste time seeing the prince off.

As Ashoka left the city, Udaya ensured that some food was sent to Somadeva that night, for only hardships and suffering were reserved for him in the coming days.

CHAPTER SEVENTEEN

A Traitor is Revealed

As Vasunaga was penning a letter in the waning light of the setting Sun, a carrier pigeon appeared in the sky and landed in his arm.

As he unfurled the piece of thin parchment containing the message, the letters belonging to an encoded writing system delivered an interesting piece of news to him.

Vasunaga immediately made his way to Nikaias and sent a man to bring Deimachus to the Bactrian general's tent.

Nikaias was busy sharpening his sword when the merchant entered his tent as the bearer of important intelligence.

"Nikaias, Ashoka has once again improved our chances of victory. A message came from my agent in Takshasila."

Nikaias put down the sword and awaited the good news. Just then, the Greek ambassador also walked into the tent with a barrage of questions aimed at Deimachus.

"I heard you received an encoded message. What news does it bear? Has Ashoka marched out of the city?"

Vasunaga smiled and replied.

"There are divisions in the army of the Prince. He recently had twenty watchtower sentinels executed because he believes that they helped you escape. Further, my man bearing our 'gifts' has reached Takshasila and has planted the seeds of doubt and discord in Ashoka's mind. He has made some repulsive decisions like imprisoning important officers of the city which create strife in the city in his absence."

"So he has left the city with his army."

"Yes, and he has left behind a defence force to protect the city. His army is weaker and will be divided. From our strong position, we shall overwhelm him. We will soon take the city."

"Then, my man shall open the gates when we reach the city," Vasunaga said confidently.

"Let us hope he is in a position to open the gates when the time comes," Deimachus countered.

"But there is no word from your emissaries who were sent to Bucephala and Alexandria on the Indus," Nikaias interjected.

"They are emissaries. Not miracle workers. We need Greek support to counter the Mauryans. When they hear about Ashoka's defeat, they will flock to our side," Deimachus assured. "When a larger Mauryan army comes to face us, we will have the numbers to fight them. But, for now, we need to stay here and let Ashoka come to us."

In Takshasila, Vasunaga's agent stood in a prison cell watching the walls blankly as he wondered about his next course of action.

When he finally snapped out of his reverie, his sight fell upon the prisoner who refused to touch his food.

"You need to eat Somadeva. If you do not eat, you will not have the strength for what we have in store for you."

Somadeva sullenly faced his captor.

"The food is poisoned is it not? I always thought it would be Vasunaga who would have me killed."

The Mauryan officer rose to his full height, his impassive eyes showing no hint of emotion.

"It is Vasunaga who will get you killed."

Somadeva's eyes widened in shock as he took in the words of the Mauryan commander.

"Why would you betray your prince?"

"Because he is not my prince," Udayaditya whispered.

Somadeva recoiled in terror as he tried to slink away from the shadow of the commander who was his greatest enemy at the moment. However, Udaya was quick to react and wrapped his bony fingers around his victim's neck.

"I do not need to poison you. I could torture you until all that is left for you is death. Or, I could give you an instant death. Either way, you die. I wanted you to have your last meal because you were once a friend of Vasunaga. That is all the courtesy I owe you."

Tears streamed down Somadeva's face as he realised his situation. Udaya released the once great merchant from his grip, confident that he had broken his detainee's resistance.

Somadeva prayed for Gautami's safety and cursed the day he met Vasunaga. Udaya watched the detainee keenly, waiting for the last meal to end for him to carry out the task of killing the man before him. Just then an eerie darkness descended upon the dungeons as all the lamps were extinguished in rapid succession. A brief silence pervaded the building until a sudden onslaught of furious footsteps reverberated across the dungeons.

In the darkness, Udaya fell quiet and alert as he carefully made his way out of the prison to find out the source behind the sudden blackness. He carefully reached the flight of the steps that led to the dungeons from the higher levels.

As he reached the base of the steps, an oil lamp placed in a wall groove was lit. That is when Udaya knew that his secret was out.

The light highlighted the contours of the Mauryan prince's face as shadows played upon his face. When the flickering flame settled, the prince's face was visible as he stood glaring at his commander'. As the other lamps were lit again, Udaya noticed how his men who were posted as guards of the prison were either incapacitated or outright killed without making a sound. Thunder whipped and cracked outside. Twenty Mauryan warriors were armoured, unlike the ordinary Mauryan soldier, and well-armed with swords, daggers, clubs and spears. A well-built man with streaming black hair that fell to his shoulders stood next to the prison cell where Somadeva was imprisoned.

"Udaya, I am sure you have met Prabhakara. He is the protégé of Dharmasena, specially trained to be invisible. Anybody can kill and protect. But Prabhakara can do it from the shadows. He is the leader of an elite unit of warriors loyal only to me. Answerable only to me."

"So, he is my replacement," Udaya asked coolly.

"No. You work for the Mauryan Crown but are loyal to Vasunaga. Prabhakara is loyal only to me, like Dharmasena."

Udaya stood there staring at the prince. The others stood around him, keeping a keen eye on him, waiting for him to make a mistake. But Udaya had already made his move.

"You are too late. Somadeva is already dead. I snapped his neck."

Prabhakara cast a glance into the prison cell and noticed the body of the merchant slumped against the wall.

"I do not care about Somadeva or his life. I needed proof that you were the traitor which I have now," Ashoka remarked.

Udaya was quiet as Prabhakara quickly knocked out the renegade commander.

When Udaya regained consciousness, he was bound in a prison cell overlooked by five warriors of Ashoka's elite unit.

A rare smile spread as he realised that Ashoka had intentionally lured him into the dungeon by giving him charge over Somadeva's interrogation. By disguising Dharmasena as the prince and feigning his absence in Takshasila, Ashoka led Udaya to drop his guard and reveal his secrets to Somadeva. Meanwhile, the prince made his way to the dungeons when Udayaditya revealed his secrets, confirming his betrayal.

What he did not understand was how the prince began suspecting his commanders.

It did not matter. Udaya would never know.

He raised his head to find Ashoka on the other side of the cell.

"You will be hung once I return from the battle. Do not fret, I will have the head of your master in tow with me."

Udaya remained silent and did not respond. The prince stood staring at the renegade and when he realised he wasn't going to elicit any response, he walked away, switching his focus to the oncoming battle.

However, before leaving the city to join Dharmasena, Ashoka reached Khara's prison cell where the garrison captain stood perplexed.

"Forgive me, Khara. Normally, I would not have arrested you."

"Your Highness?"

"The spies of our enemies are everywhere. I wanted them to report discord among our army ranks and discontent against me in Takshasila to our enemies. That would make our enemies drop their guard. I knew someone would report my faults and mishandling of situations to our enemies. Making a show of arresting the garrison captain of the city and executing my own soldiers spell incompetence. But, I did not think it would be Udayaditya, my own commander and an officer who has served me for years who would be one of the spies."

Khara detected a slight tremor in the otherwise strong voice of the prince.

"I need you to take over the defence of the city once again, Khara."

"You executed your own soldiers," a shocked Khara asked.

"No. It was all just a show like I just said. The soldiers are safe. I wanted to ensure that the soldiers were supposedly executed on the outskirts of the city. This was to make certain that the roving eyes of the common citizenry would not witness the incident, but persistent spies would turn up at the place of the incident to observe the occurrence. And that is exactly what happened. For good measure, I tracked Udayaditya's movements after my suspicion was roused about his loyalty. My spy reported that Udayaditya sent a secret message to his master possibly containing the latest happenings in the city. But, their plans will backfire. Possibly they wished to destroy my army from within through Udaya. But, I shall use their misunderstanding against them. For that, I need you to watch over the city while I am gone. With you watching over the city, I can crush our enemies."

Khara was taken aback. He remained quiet, but after a moment, he walked out of the prison cell and put his right hand to his chest.

"I will protect this city in the name of the Empire. Rest assured, as long as I live, no enemy shall set foot in Takshasila."

Ashoka smiled and marched out of the dungeon. A small unit of soldiers headed by Prabhakara waited for him outside the Governor's Palace. The prince joined them and soon marched out of the city to join Dharmasena and the main army.

As Ashoka marched away from the city he was sent to protect, I slept fitfully that night, unaware of the impending battle that would be fought for the city's future.

CHAPTER EIGHTEEN

THE MARCH TO THE ENEMY

Under cover of night, Ashoka's army quickly covered the ground as he led his forces towards the mountain pass from where the Bactrians had entered Gandhara. Centuries ago, the great Darius of the Achaemenid empire had entered Bharatvarsha through the very same mountain pass and had quickly seized Gandhara to make it a part of his intercontinental empire. The gold that had flowed from Gandhara had enriched the Achaemenid empire beyond its wildest expectations. The Greeks had inherited the region from the Persians when Alexander marched into India after conquering the Achaemenids. Alexander's main force had also entered India through the mountain Pass, while Alexander himself led a smaller unit through a route further north, where he came upon the city of Aornos, near Mansehra and laid siege to it. After facing some initial difficulties, Alexander conquered the city and finally reunited with the main force near Takshasila in the spring season.

However, the invaders rearing to face Ashoka were a different lot. While they entered Bharatvarsha through the pass, they did not march ahead to Takshasila to conquer it. They decided to set up camp a little distance away from the pass in an open valley and awaited their enemy. They decided that the best way to fight Ashoka was to meet his forces in open battle and rout his army with their superior numbers. Functioning under the belief that Udayaditya was in charge of Takshasila's defences, they would take the city without bloodshed.

Their battle plan involved Deimachus with his Greek cavalry on the army's left flank along with the new Bactrian levies, while the seasoned Bactrian infantry modelled after the Macedonian phalanx would be the vanguard backed by the light armoured horse archers who served as the rearguard of the army. Nikaias would lead his elite horsemen on the right flank. His cavalry unit was heavily armoured and armed with javelins and swords. Nikaias planned to use his elite cavalry as shock troops to deal a devastating blow to Ashoka's left flank that would face Nikaias's forces. If he was lucky, he would kill the commander in the cavalry charge itself. Vasunaga and his mercenary bodyguards would remain in reserve to back the invading army in case something went wrong.

Nikaias estimated that the Mauruan army would soon be upon the Bactrians positioned in the valley. He had sent scouts to look out for the Muryan army in the night. Surprisingly, the monsoons hit Gandhara early with the clouds releasing their grim burdens upon the dry earth. As Nikaias stood inside his tent, he realised that the rains would complicate his plans. To further complicate matters, none of the scouts returned the following day. While his scouts were known to be careful, he suspected they had been caught by a reconnaissance force of the Mauryans. Either way, he kept his hopes up and awaited news from them.

As the next day passed uneventfully in the shadow of the storm clouds, the Bactrian general kept his forces ready in case the Mauryans attacked at night to gain the element of surprise. As he was discussing his final battle plans with his captains, a soldier came running in to deliver news that a Bactrian scout had returned.

Nikaias rushed out of the tent to find the scout injured and slumping upon his horse. The man was barely breathing. Nikaias quickly ordered his men to tend to the injured outrider who was barely conscious. As he was taken into one of the tents to tend to his wounds, the Bactrian general followed his men and kept a keen eye upon the wounded man. He noticed numerous cuts and scrapes on his lookout's body.

It looked like he had been dragged and hauled around by something.

Nikaias carefully examined the hands of the scout to find no marks left behind by any ligatures or ropes.

He was not bound to a horse. He had not been dragged through the mud or rocks.

His physician found that the lookout's arms and chest had been nearly crushed by someone with a powerful vice-like grip.

"General, it is difficult for this soldier to survive. I do not know how he survived for so long and made it back to the camp, but his days are numbered."

Nikaias shook his head. He walked to the unconscious scout and prodded him awake.

"Hey, Bessus, the physician here says your days are numbered. But, you can still help us by giving us the required information. Fulfil what you were sent to do. What happened?"

The scout did not respond to his general's initial calls, but finally, Nikaias's voice got through. Bessus struggled to open his eyes and mumbled something.

Nikaias brought his ears to the dying man who whispered something that shocked him.

His battle plans needed to be changed. As he marched out back to his tent, he realised that Takshasila was helping the prince by bolstering his power.

He had wasted a few precious hours waiting for the scout to deliver his message. He had to make changes in his battle tactics. Another night was upon the invaders and thunder resounded across the heavens. Lightening occasionally lit up the pitch-black skies.

The captains who waited for their general in the tent witnessed how the confidence of the Bactrian was shaken up. Vasunaga and Deimachus were summoned once again.

Vasunaga and Deimachus were soon to arrive at the scene.

"Prince Ashoka is bringing elephants to the battlefield! Our scouts were killed by those monsters, the sound of whose movements were suppressed by the storm and heavy downpour. Before our scouts realised, the elephants were upon them. Ashoka found them somehow before they could locate his army. It means he knows where our camp is located and is marching upon us. We do not know how many elephants the enemy has, but we must expect that there will be enough to rout our army."

The captains murmured among themselves and faced their commander for his orders.

"Our formation remains the same. But, the light cavalry will form the vanguard while the infantry will be in the rear. With suitable cavalry tactics, we can have our horses distract the elephant corps which will most likely form the main centre of the Mauryan army to charge and crush our army's centre. Alexander's horses proved that Porus's elephants could be brought down. We shall do the same. Relay these plans to the rest of the army. We need to get our army in formation and prepared for the battle."

The captains soon dispersed with only Deimachus and Vasunaga remaining in the general's tent.

Nikaias menacingly strode to Vasunaga and wrapped his hand around the merchant's neck.

"Your man and your merchants have sided with Ashoka," he growled. "He is the one who conveyed our location to the Mauryan Prince. We have been betrayed."

Vasunaga struggled as Deimachus stood witness to the fear that rapidly spread across his face.

"Udaya...will never...betray...us. He hates...the Mauryans," Vasunaga choked on his words. "He would never...talk."

"Udaya has been in the service of Ashoka for years. He has been turned," Nikaias retaliated.

Deimachus shook himself out of his stupor and pulled Nikaias away from Vasunaga who gasped and coughed, his lungs gratefully accepting the gift of oxygen once again.

"Keep your cool, Nikaias. We need you to be calm if you are going to lead us to victory. It could have been our captured soldiers who revealed everything. Believe me, Ashoka is a master interrogator."

"They were sent there to help his man take the city in case of any opposition. Instead, if Ashoka marches upon us with elephants, it means that my men are either dead or as good as dead."

Nikaias stomped out of the tent, leaving the Greek ambassador to handle the Indian.

"Vasunaga, if Ashoka has elephants, it cannot all have come from the garrison. How well trained are the elephants of the Takshasila Merchant Guild?"

"Our elephants are trained both as beasts of burden and as defenders of our goods caravans. They are not war elephants but can hold their ground. They are kept afraid of fire though which renders them berserk."

"The monsoons will not allow us to harness fire," Deimachus mulled. "How could we have not foreseen this?"

"I had taken measures to sow seeds of distrust between the Mauryans and the merchants. Further, Ashoka himself did a good job playing the role of tyrant. Perhaps, Ashoka is marching upon us with merely a handful of elephants from the garrison."

"Or he has the might of all the elephants of Takshasila," Deimachus presented an alternate view.

Vasunaga's eyes widened as a thought crossed his mind. The look did not escape Deimachus.

"What is it?"

"Indrabahu, that traitor," Vasunaga hissed, slumping on the floor. "He has convinced the merchants to ally with Ashoka. He has used the journals of Jhadamitra."

"What are you talking about?"

"Jhadamitra was the last Setti of the Takshasila Merchant Guild. The man was shrewd beyond measure. He had secretly loaned money to Chanakya to raise an army against Emperor Dhana Nanda. But Chanakya needed to first convince Jhadamitra that his candidate, Chandragupta Maurya had the royal blood and valid reasons to defeat Dhana Nanda. Further, Jhadamitra was promised exclusive trading rights in the Gangetic plains to the Setti in return for the sums of money, which enriched the Guild. However, Jhadamitra also knew Chanakya's most closely held secret, something that convinced the entire Bharatavarsha that Chandragupta Maurya had the legitimacy to be crowned sovereign of the land you call India."

Deimachus grew interested by the minute.

"Chanakya had everyone convinced that through a special ritual, the deities had granted favour in the form of uncountable wealth to Chanakya which allowed him to raise an army of mercenaries to take Dhana Nanda down. Meanwhile, Chanakya portrayed Chandragupta as the last descendant of the Kshatriya clan of Pipphalivana, a kingdom that Dhana Nanda had conquered by deceit and ruthlessly destroyed to the last brick. The people of Pipphalivana were enslaved and made to mine iron, limestone and copper from the plateaus in Magadha. This enriched Dhana Nanda and he did not pay a single penny to the slaves. Further, he ensured that trading rights in his kingdom and the neighbouring kingdoms within his influence were given to his loyalists and the Takshasila Merchant Guild suffered. These were the circumstances that made Jhadamitra invest in Chanakya."

"So what went wrong," Deimachus asked.

"Chanakya did not keep up his support for long. Initially, after Dhana Nanda's defeat and the crowning of Chandragupta as the first Mauryan Emperor, Chanakya had his protégé grant the agreed favours to the Takshasila Merchant Guild. But, over the years, the Guild became too powerful and rich. It threatened the Empire with Gandhara virtually falling into the hands of the merchants. With Chanakya alarmed at the Guild's rapid growth, he started creating obstacles for the Guild. That is when Jhadamitra revealed to Chanakya the journals which not only contained the financial dealings between the crooked Brahmin and the merchants but also the very secret behind

Chandragupta's legitimacy as a Kshatriya."

Deimachus grew excited as he waited for the big revelation.

"Chandragupta was no Kshatriya and neither was he a prince of Pipphalivana. He was a person of low birth, a boy whose parents sold peacock feathers for a living in the markets of Magadha. That boy from a poor household was made the king of one of the largest empires of Bharatavarsha. He had no legitimacy other than the false ancestry circulated by that crafty Brahmin. Nobody knows what the last prince of the Pipphalivana looked like because Dhana Nanda had destroyed everything. So, Chandragupta 'Maurya' was propped up in his place."

Deimachus had suspected that this was the big secret that Jhadamitra had held as a weapon against Chanakya when the recounting of the past began. But, he was still taken aback by the measures undertaken by the kingmaker to depose Dhana Nanda, a man supposedly of low birth himself and replace him with another man with no royal blood. But, Deimachus was not a man who gave in to mere suspicions and beliefs.

"Is there any evidence of Emperor Chandragupta's low birth other than the claims of Setti Jhadamitra?"

"People do not need evidence. Chanakya presented no evidence when he claimed that Chandragupta was the prince of Pipphalivana. But, it doesn't matter anymore. Indrabahu must have surrendered the journals to Ashoka in return for protecting the merchants. Further, he must have loaned the Guild's elephants to extend support to the Prince. We need to somehow overcome Ashoka."

"I should get going. You need to prepare your men. Your men will be the reserves."

As Deimachus left to consult with the head of his cavalry unit, Vasunaga realised that defeat at Mauryan hands was a possibility.

CHAPTER NINETEEN

THE BATTLE FOR TAKSHASILA BEGINS

As Khara took over the defences of the city, he found the twenty soldiers whom Ashoka had supposedly executed. The twenty guards were given stern warnings and were sent back to their respective positions. Udayaditya's men were arrested and imprisoned and Somadeva's body was handed over to Indrabahu who promised to oversee his funeral rites. Further, Indrabahu who knew the truth about Somadeva, promised to clear his name among the citizens of the city.

Akshaya and I watched as Mauryan soldiers were dispersed throughout the city. The garrison was completely emptied except for a few guards to oversee the prisoners. They would be punished by Ashoka when he returned.

Meanwhile, the Mauryan governor was relieved of his duties and position. He welcomed the orders and requested that he be sent back to Pataliputra as soon as possible. He was finally exhausted with Takshasila.

Classes had been suspended at the University for a few weeks now. The city seemed different without the debates at every odd corner and the chants of the Buddhists and Brahmins. The people still harboured respect for Suryanaga as the monk comforted the people and assured them that if Vasunaga was guilty, his deeds would not go unpunished. Something told me that we would soon find out.

Meanwhile, as a new day dawned upon the valley that would soon be transformed into a battlefield, even the red Sun showed its face among the great billow of black clouds, giving their swollen frames crimson hued edges. As Nikaias oversaw the formation of his army, he finally heard the roaring trumpets of the elephants in the distance. Soon, Ashoka's army was visible on the horizon as the dust kicked up the horses and the elephants rose up in the air.

Nikaias's scouts reported that Ashoka's troops had stopped marching and were setting up camp some distance away.

"How many elephants?"

"Approximately thirty, My Lord."

"We can deal with thirty elephants. Continue keeping an eye on them."

Nikaias tried to play out the possible battle scenarios in his mind.

If Ashoka's elephants charged at his main centre to rout his cavalry, his light cavalry would need to break the formation lines and scatter to distract the elephants. This would allow his Bactrian phalanx to attack the distracted elephants from behind and harass the behemoths by using their sarrisas or the long pikes and their swords to hack at the elephants' trunks and cause distress to the animals. When the elephants were put to flight, they would cause immense chaos within the Mauryan army. The flanks would be dealt with by Deimachus and Nikaias's troops and the Mauryan archers would be put to flight by the light cavalry composed of horse archers.

An alternate scenario was if the elephants were protected by Mauryan foot soldiers, his horse archers would ride close and aim for the infantry. When the elephants charged forward to counter the volley of arrows, the cavalry would break formation and the phalanx would simply make way and allow the beasts to pass. Once the beasts had passed, the horse archers would regroup and pick out the Mauryan archers while the phalanx would move in on the scattered Mauryan infantry. Meanwhile, Deimachus's cavalry and Nikaias's heavy cavalry would counter the respective flanks of the Mauryan army and rout them in battle. If Deimachus fell short, his flank would be supplemented by the Bactrian infantry in the main line or the heavy cavalry in the right flank.

As Nikaias assured himself that victory was possible, his army finally stood in formation with its sights on Gandhara.

Ashoka's army was also divided into two flanks and the main centre. Ashoka equally distributed his cavalry between the left and right flanks which were headed by Dharmasena and Ashoka respectively. Dharmasena also had some infantrymen to support his cavalrymen and back up their charge. Prabhakara would lead the central vanguard consisting largely of infantrymen with long-range archers backing them up. Ashoka's elephants were positioned in front of the central infantry to destroy the Bactrian main line in a charge. The battle for Takshasila would be the greatest challenge of his young military career.

Before the great battle, Nikaias rode in front of the battle lines inspiring them to conquer the golden land that lay before them.

"Fellow lions of Bactria, before us lies a land of riches and innumerable wealth. Look around you, at your brothers in arms. Each one of you has the strength of a hundred men and an unyielding spirit.

The enemy may be strong, but we shall rout them from the battlefield and send them to their deaths. Their people yearn to be connected to the greater cultures of the mighty Greek civilisations of the West. It is for this reason that the honourable merchant prince, Vasunaga of this land has invited us and we shall liberate him and his people from the oppression of the Mauryan Crown.

The great Alexander crossed the Hydaspes River, but could not advance enough to conquer beyond the land known as Paropamsidae. His dream of conquering the great land known as India was left unfulfilled. However, the great powers vest in us the power to succeed where Alexander failed.

As we march into battle, let the roar of our voices shake the very earth. Let the clash of our swords be the thunder that heralds our victory. We are unstoppable and invincible.

Together, we will conquer and triumph. Now, let us establish the Bactrian empire in India."

A roar of approval rose in the air as the Bactrian warriors stomped their feet and beat their shields energetically. The horses neighed furiously and reared to answer the winds' call that blew indignantly, attempting to raise dust on the battlefield.

Despite being positioned some distance away, the Mauryan army heard the battle cries of the Bactrians.

"These Yavanas think they can take our lands away from us. Let us show them why enemies fear the steel of Bharatvarsha."

A thunderous cry rose from the Mauryan ranks as the elephants trumpeted in fury and shook the earth with their formidable stomping. It was like the battlefield was suddenly gripped by a powerful earthquake.

With the valley resounding with the battle cries, Nikaias and Ashoka ordered their respective armies to attack.

Ashoka's elephants were quick to act; their mahouts urged them to charge ahead. The mighty quadrupeds rushed ahead of the main line in a coordinated manner. The Bactrian horsemen quickly reacted and rose to meet the charge.

Ashoka witnessed the central troops move slowly after the charge of the elephants under the orders of Prabhakara. However, there was no movement on the right flank of the Mauryan army. Meanwhile, on the far side of the valley, Dharmasena had issued the orders for his units to move on the left flank of the Mauryan army.

Nikaias's heavily armoured cavalry watched the horse archers ride ahead, meet the elephant charge, and commence their own charge towards the Mauryan army's left flank. As the Bactrian phalanx began its own steady march against the defenders, Deimachus experienced Greeks however, stood their ground and made the new levies do the same. They decided to meet Ashoka's charge only when his units moved without proactively riding to his side of the field.

As different parts of both armies moved to confront each other, the Bactrian phalanx was surprised when Deimachus's Greek riders crashed into the infantry with devastating effect. Their coherent ranks were scattered as Deimachus's two hundred horsemen cut through the formation like a hot knife through butter.

In the sound of battle, Nikaias did not realise his phalanx was compromised. The clueless levies did not understand what happened and broke formation to flee. The horse riders scattered in time to allow the elephants to make their way to the Bactrian infantry. Unknown to the horse archers, the elephants made their way to the phalanx which was no longer an orderly unit of disciplined soldiers. It was a scattered mass of betrayed individuals who were soon trampled under the feet of rampaging elephants and killed in great numbers. Deimachus quickly led his forces away from the chaos and pursued the fleeing levies. The galloping horsemen soon cut down the inexperienced novices.

Meanwhile, Nikaias's heavy cavalry soon clashed against Dharmasena's military units. The resulting collisions almost caused Dharmasena to fall off his horse. As he fought off the invaders with his sword, his unarmoured infantry unit hoarded casualties as the armoured cavalrymen hacked away at them. The clangour of steel against steel caused Dharmasena to fight harder as his men fell one by one to the Bactrians. Dharmasena's cavalry tried to stop the advance of the Bactrian right flank, but they were losing ground until Dharmasena finally gave the order for them to retreat.

As the Bactrian horse archers regrouped to take out the Mauryan infantry, they were met with a volley of arrows from the Mauryan archers who protected the rear of the infantrymen. While the volley did initially take Bactrian lives, it barely did anything to slow down their momentum. The horse archers were soon upon the Mauryan infantrymen of the centre who under Prabhakara's orders retreated to prevent confrontation. The Mauryans raised their massive shields and continued to withdraw, while the

Bactrian horse archers slowed down their charge and let loose their own volley of arrows from their composite bows which were different from the Mauryan longbows. Further, the Bactrian archers were trained to shoot while riding horses, giving them more mobility than traditional archers in Bharatvarsha.

As the horse archers continued showering arrows upon the Mauryans, Prabhakara's men did not engage and started taking casualties. As Prabhakara's men were losing ground and retreating, their ranks swelled with soldiers from Ashoka's units. In the heat of the battle, the Bactrian horse archers failed to notice Ashoka leading his cavalry to encircle the Bactrian light cavalry and attack them from behind. The horse archers turned to find their rear completely vulnerable and under attack. As they tried to change tactics and retreat to join Nikaias's heavy cavalry, they were shocked to find their route blocked by Deimachus's Greek cavalry which had completed its massacre of the Bactrian levies.

Completely boxed in from all sides, the Bactrian light cavalry fought for survival as the Mauryans and Greeks tightened their chokehold on the horse archers and attacked them from all sides.

When Nikaias finally realised what had transpired with his central phalanx and the troops of the invading army's left flank, he directed his units to rush and protect the surviving central cavalry units. As Nikaias's forces neared the Greek troops, Dharmasena quickly rallied his own cavalry troops and directed them to destroy Nikaias's cavalry from the rear.

As Nikaias and Dharmasena led their respective cavalries into what was now a convoluted rabble of Bactrians, Mauryans and Greeks, the resulting chaos threatened to destroy both armies with no clear victor or loser.

However, Nikaias's army had already sustained heavy casualties with his phalanx, levies and main troops routed in battle. Nikaias was not one to flee, however, when his cavalrymen attacked the Greek horsemen, who were busy making short work of the Bactrian horse archers, Dharmasena's mounted troops swiftly joined the fray to hack away at Nikaias's men and their steed.

The fighting went on until the curtains of darkness fell upon the bloody battlefield.

Bodies of men and beasts lay strewn on the battlefield with the odd wails of pain and anguish filling the air. The survivors lay shackled and awaited imprisonment at the hands of their foreign captors. While both sides sustained casualties, the Bactrian army was no more. Nikaias himself was in chains, too bloodied and bruised to be conscious. While Dharmasena and Prabhakara oversaw the medical treatment of the wounded at the hands of the accompanying physicians, the surviving Greeks were inspected by Deimachus and his captain.

Meanwhile, Ashoka rode with some soldiers to capture Vasunaga, the one who had invited trouble to Gandhara. Nikaias had claimed the legitimacy to attack Gandhara at the invitation of the merchant prince.

However, when Ashoka reached the spot where the reserves of the invading army were positioned, he found the survivors rounded up with the majority of them trampled under the feet of the elephants.

Ashoka scoured the place for Vasunaga, but he found the man missing.

"Where is Vasunaga," he asked the leader of the mahouts who had led the elephant charge against the

Bactrians.

"Your Highness, we searched high and low for him, but it seems that he fled with a few trusted men."

"How did he escape? We have routed the Bactrians. We have captured their general. Their army has been annihilated. But we let the mastermind of this entire battle slip out of our grasp, right under our noses."

He barked orders to his captain to send a unit to Takshasila as quickly as possible if Vasunaga was travelling to Takshasila, though the situation seemed unlikely. Similarly, he ordered another unit to make its way to the frontiers of Gandhara to ensure that Vasunaga did not enter the Greek or Bactrian empire. However, precious time was lost in the relay of these orders, which would determine whether Vasunaga escaped the Mauryan clutches.

Ashoka wanted to parade Nikaias, Vasunaga and Udayaditya in front of the Gandharan citizens of Takshasila to show them that one of their own was working with foreign invaders and that he was fair enough to punish his own soldiers if they were discovered to be traitors.

However, if Vasunaga was not found, he would make do with a public display of bestowing mercy and forgiveness upon the senior officers of the Takshasila Merchant Guild who had conspired with the traitorous Vasunaga to overthrow the Mauryan crown in Gandhara. He would make sure that the future generations believed this battle to be a civil war where Takshasila had risen up in arms against the Mauryans and the Mauryan prince had been magnanimous to forgive the conspirators behind the dastardly attack on the Crown. All was fair in love, war and politics.

CHAPTER TWENTY

A BATTLE WON AND THE LOOMING WAR

Ashoka's men never found Vasunaga. The merchant prince had fled the battlefield when Ashoka was busy fighting Nikaias. After two days of coordinating search parties, Ashoka finally decided to return to Takshasila. He still had Nikaias and Udayaditya to punish. Before returning to Takshasila, Ashoka addressed the doubts of the Mauryan captains about Deimachus's loyalty.

From the very beginning, Deimachus had decided to side with the Mauryans. When Udayaditya had returned to Takshasila with some prisoners, Deimachus had ensured that a trusted man of his, in the form of a prisoner, carried a message to Ashoka containing the truth about Udayaditya and the location of the invaders. While Ashoka had his doubts about Deimachus's claims, Udayaditya's betrayal while preparing to kill Somadeva convinced the prince that Deimachus's words carried the truth. Finally, Deimachus's attack on the Bactrian phalanx and the levies played a major contribution to Ashoka's victory over the invaders.

When the Mauryan army returned to Takshasila, the soldiers were welcomed as heroes. I was in the crowd of cheering citizens when I witnessed the historic moment where Ashoka rode into the city, at the head of his victorious army, with the Bactrian prisoners in tow. At that moment, I believed that the Mauryan prince's splendour was no lesser than the Mauryan emperor's himself.

I was also surprised to see the return of Ambassador Deimachus who was followed by his Greek riders. Ashoka was warmly received by a welcoming party on the premises of the Great Meeting Hall of Takshasila. He stood upon an artificially constructed platform with the other victors, where the luminaries of the city heaped praises upon the Mauryan prince, hailing him as the saviour of Gandhara. I was proud to see that Haridasa was a part of the welcoming party, standing close to Ambassador Deimachus as if they were old friends.

When the Mauryan army had been away, Takshasila witnessed eventful days. The city received word of a Mauryan traitor and the release of Captain Khara, who had been arrested on the orders of Prince Ashoka for being a suspected deserter. Not only was Captain Khara released, he was also left in charge of the city's defences in the absence of Ashoka. Fortunately, there had been no attack. The citizens were also shocked to hear from the defunct Administrative Council that Somadeva, the Gandhara traitor had been framed for the assassination attempt on the Mauryan governor, the assassination of the assailant behind the attempt on the governor and the offences of spreading terror in the city. The real mastermind had always been Vasunaga.

Somadeva was given a quiet cremation, which was not attended by many people. Among the people close to him, Gautami, his former wife had also been present at the scene, silently wondering what life would have been with him if she had never become a bhikkhuni.

While the citizens were celebrating Ashoka's victory, the prince who had silently stood, receiving praise from the luminary, finally spoke up.

"Citizens of Gandhara and the Mauryan Empire, we will have time to celebrate the victory of the Empire over its enemies. However, there is something to be done before we commence the celebration."

On his orders, his guards brought a bound Nikaias and Udayaditya onto the platform, where they were made to kneel and await the Crown's justice. My gaze was fixed upon Udayaditya, who once again struck me as familiar.

"The enemies of and traitors to the Empire and Bharatvarsha shall be executed in the name of the Mauryan Crown. But, Commander Udayaditya has served the Empire and this great country faithfully before the great betrayal for several years. Therefore, I give him a chance to plead for mercy."

Udaya glared at the citizens with bloodshot eyes and sniggered.

"The Mauryans have spread their empire to every corner of Bharatvarsha, except Kalinga and the deep south. They have stolen land and destroyed homes. You foolish men and women have willingly surrendered your city to them," he cackled like a madman. "I am in no position to criticise you because my people had surrendered our village in the south out of fear of their chariots and elephants. They burnt my village and all the surrounding fields. The fire that destroyed my world threatened to burn the very skies that day."

The people noticed how Udaya seemed lost when recounting the destruction of his village at the hands of the Mauryan army.

"I failed to protect my brother and I failed to protect my freedom. I was finally freed by Vasunaga who gave me a chance to witness the atrocities heaped by the Empire upon the people of Bharatvarsha. I was part of the massacre of the dacoits of Vidisha and the proud warriors of the Vrijj confederacy. The dacoits were anti-social elements, but the warriors of the Vriji were the protectors of their Gana Sangha. We did not take any prisoners. Instead, we put them all to death. They were proud ancient people who brought Emperor Ajatashatru to his knees with their adamance. So, we massacred their warriors through deceit. I am a barbaric soldier of the Mauryan Army and I deserve to die," Udaya declared, turning to glare at Ashoka and spat.

While the people were quiet, Ashoka was unmoved. He brought his hand down in a gesture to order the execution. I watched as an executioner swiftly brought a sharp sword down upon Udaya's neck, severing his head from the rest of the body in one swoop. Fortunately, people stood away from the condemned man and as his blood soaked the platform, I felt a tear from my cheek.

I realised that my guardian, Abhaya at the Kalinga Vihara would never meet his brother who was lost when the Mauryans raided his village in the south all those years ago. I wondered if Udaya was not bound, would anybody be able to lay a hand upon him? Probably Dharmasena and Prabhakara would probably be able to. But, would anybody be able to kill him? Would the grim prince of the Mauryans be able to kill him? I remembered every detail of the story narrated by Abhaya about two boys forcibly taken away from their home by a war that they never wanted to wage. The brothers may have been different people, but their characteristically sharp features and intelligent eyes spoke volumes about the common blood that they shared.

Unlike Udaya's execution which was met by an awkward silence from the people, Nikaias's execution was met by wild cheers from the people. Ashoka promised that Bactria would pay for violating the borders of Gandhara with blood and gold and the people cheered. The prince also announced that there would be celebrations held at the Governor's Palace and soon a new governor would be appointed to take over the administration of Gandhara.

I caught Dharmasena standing with a bowed head, his gaze fixed upon the headless body of Udayaditya. Perhaps, there was regret in the Mauryan army.

The crowd soon followed Ashoka as he made his way to the Governor's Palace with his officers. Ashoka's last orders before his exit were that Udaya's and Nikaias bodies were to be handled with care and their funeral rites were to be conducted with respect. Dharmasena undertook the task of having the bloody mess cleaned on the platform. Following his prince's orders, he had Udaya's and Nikaias's bodies handled with care. As Dharmasena was overseeing everything, I walked up to him and a smile spread on his face.

"Samudra, the victorious Prince Ashoka has left for the Governor's Palace. You will find him there."

"I am not here for that, Commander. I am here for Commander Udayaditya."

An inquiring look came upon Dharmasena's face.

"What do you have to do with Commander Udayaditya?"

I did not hesitate to share the connection between Udayaditya and Abhaya in Kalinga. That got Dharmasena thinking.

"Even if I sent a message to Abhaya inviting him to Takhshasila or had the body of Udaya sent to Kalinga, Abhaya would only see the rotting body of his brother."

"I did not say do not hold the funeral rites until Abhaya arrives or send his body to Kalinga for the funeral rites. Hold the funeral rites, but whatever earthly possessions Commander Udayaditya had should be handed over to his brother. That includes his ashes. That would tell Abhaya something about the life his brother led under the aegis of the Mauryan Empire."

Dharmasena nodded his assent and promised to fulfil my request. I thanked him and walked away to find Akshaya. I found my friend talking to Deimachus. The Greek ambassador was animatedly chatting about Emperor Antiochus's trade policies with India when he saw me appear.

"Oh, there you are, Samudra," Akshaya said. "Ambassador Deimachus is finally leaving for Pataliputra tomorrow."

The news shared by Akshaya raised the spirit of melancholy within me. I did not know when my dream of visiting Alexandria would be fulfilled. But, only Abhaya's sorry plight occupied my mind. My former guardian had lost everything in his life and gained a family in the form of the Kalinga Buddhist Sangha. How would he feel when he received his deceased brother's ashes and earthly possessions? I prayed to the deities above to give him the strength and courage to bear the bad news.

Sensing I was lost, Akshaya snapped me back into reality.

"Hey Samudra, you have brought up Alexandria even once since you came here. What is going on in that head of yours?"

"Lord Deimachus, do you believe Commander Udayaditya was a traitor to Bharatvarsha," I asked the Greek ambassador unemotionally.

"Prince Ashoka answered the question, dear Samudra. He was a traitor to the Mauryan Empire."

"When Prince Ashoka entered the city of Takshasila, he had Commander Dharmasena and Commander Udayaditya by his side, as if they were his two arms. Then Prince Ashoka branded him a traitor to the Empire and Bharatvarsha. I asked you whether you believed Udayaditya was a traitor to Bharatvarsha."

"You heard what Udayaditya declared in front of all the citizens. He sided with Vasunaga and the Bactrians to conquer Gandhara."

"That made him a traitor to Bharatvarsha? Is the Mauryan Empire synonymous with Bharatvarsha?"

"Yes, Samudra. Today the Mauryans hold power in the country and their empire is synonymous with the country. Tomorrow someone else will have their empire synonymous with Bharatvarsha. Countries belong to the ones in power, but power is never held by one forever. But, today the Mauryans hold power in this country."

I did not like Deimachus's answer. I realised that the Greek ambassador himself had betrayed the Bactrians and Vasunaga because Prince Ashoka held the power in Gandhara. With Ashoka indebted to the Greeks, Deimachus ensured that he had cultivated a long-standing alliance with the Mauryan prince who would certainly sit on the Mauryan throne one day. At that moment, I realised that the one who held power could reshape the world to his or her liking. However, power corrupts even the strongest of wills. Even a benevolent person under the influence of power could turn into a tyrant.

I couldn't stand there any longer. I immediately walked away much to the surprise of Deimachus and Akshaya.

I reached home and was greeted by Varaprada who immediately noticed my serious demeanour.

Her inquisitive gaze was enough for me to spill my guts to her.

"You have been through a lot and have come so far in life. Maybe, you can help your guardian, Abhaya, achieve some closure, if he needs it. Once the funeral rites are over, why don't you undertake a journey to Kalinga and spend some time there? It would do you some good."

Just as they were talking, a Mauryan soldier appeared at their doorstep.

"Lord Dharmasena has summoned you to be present during the funeral rites of Commander Udayaditya which is to be held tomorrow on the outskirts of the city. The funeral rites will be held at daybreak."

"Summoned or invited," I asked, just to make sense of the orders.

"I mentioned the word summoned," the soldier retorted scathingly. "He is the commander of the forces of Prince Ashoka, Saviour of Gandhara. Even an invitation from him is to be treated as a summons."

I bowed courteously to the soldier and accepted the 'summons'. The soldier hurriedly left, his other duties awaiting him.

The rest of the day was uneventful and the next day soon dawned upon Takshasila, a city free from immediate danger.

As I reached the spot where Commander Udayaditya's funeral rites were to take place, a few others had already arrived. The majority of them were Mauryan soldiers and soon Dharmasena too reached the spot. I found Prabhakara following him, keeping a close eye on the surroundings.

The arrangements for the pyre had already been made. Four soldiers behind Prabhakara carried the corpse of the deceased. Once the deceased was respectfully placed on the pyre, I was surprised to find Prince Ashoka reaching the scene with a few captains. He expected Ashoka to be the last person here.

As a few pundits recited the mantras to ensure the smooth travel of the atma to the higher realms, the pundits directed Dharmasena to light the pyre and pray to release Udayaditya's atma from the bonds of the earthly realm.

I saw Dharmasena shed a tear as he lit the pyre. The flames roared and rose to claim the body and soon Udayaditya's proud, strong and scarred body ceased to exist in the world.

As the Sun made its way up the morning sky, the flames had turned the corpse to ash and only their embers remained. While I was lost in thought, a visitor intruded upon my thinking space. When I came back to reality, I noticed Prince Ashoka standing in front of me, eyeing me curiously. I staggered a few steps back to put some distance between us.

"So, you are the boy from Kalinga who was adopted by a Buddhist Vihara?"

"So, you are a Prince of the Mauryan Empire," I asked him foolishly.

A spark of amusement flickered to life in the cold eyes of the prince.

"Yes. I am Prince Ashoka of the Mauryan Empire," he said with a mischievous twinkle in his eye.

His answer was an attempt to make the situation lighter, but my defiance grew in the face of his amusement.

Is it because you are a Prince of the Mauryan Empire that you can go around warring and killing innocents?

However, my thoughts were never put into words.

"Dharmasena told me that you know the sibling of Udayaditya."

I managed a weak nod.

"Good. Dharmasena wishes to leave for Kalinga tomorrow and wants you to accompany him. Commander Dharmasena has been loyal to me for years and he deserves to do what he feels is right. I believe you will accompany him then?"

Words still did not escape from my mouth. Responses eluded me. Ashoka awaited an answer, impatience steadily creeping into his face.

Just then the rain deities showered their grace upon me. While black clouds gathered in the sky as the cremation rituals commenced, the rains finally made their way to the earth as the soldiers finished collecting the ashes of the deceased Mauryan commander.

"I will go with Commander Dharmasena to Kalinga," I answered with renewed assurance when Ashoka turned his gaze to the skies.

The prince heard my answer.

"Good."

He turned to leave, when finally a question rolled out of my tongue.

"What about you, Your Highness? What will you do from here onwards?"

Ashoka took some time to think.

"I will be leaving for Pataliputra today with Lord Deimachus. Your city is safe with Captain Khara until the Mauryan Crown appoints a new Governor for Gandhara. I believe the Emperor will send me to quash a rebellion elsewhere or bring another lawless district under the protection of Mauryan law."

"But, you are the Saviour of Gandhara. What about a reward," I asked inquisitively.

Ashoka laughed. It was a roaring laugh that resounded despite the thundering clouds in the sky.

"The Mauryan Emperor is not a man who thinks along ordinary lines. He will never reward his sons for something so trivial. Until I do not vanquish Lord Indra himself and bring Swarga under Mauryan rule. Maybe then, Emperor Bindusara will be pleased enough to make me the governor of a distant part of the Empire."

As a person who never knew my father, I did not understand the relationship between Emperor Bindusara and Prince Ashoka, but I certainly did not want to be in Ashoka's place.

I bowed low courteously and watched as Ashoka sought cover from the rains which were pouring now. I stood alone in the rain wondering about my prospective journey to Kalinga.

CHAPTER TWENTY-ONE

THE RETURN TO THE KALINGA VIHARA

<u>Two years later</u>

In my distant memories, I could see Askshaya and myself climbing up that hill overlooking the great city of Takshasila. But, those memories were relegated to my dreams now.

In the two years that had passed since the war for Takshasila, Akshaya had stepped up to help out his father in his prospering business. My friend who used to huff and puff when climbing hills was travelling to cities situated along the Uttarapatha. The last I heard, he was in Ujjain trying to establish a foothold in the cotton trade in the city on behalf of his father.

While Akshaya's father, Dhananjaya was still a part of the Takshasila Merchant Guild, the power of the guild was steadily on the decline. Prince Ashoka had kept his word and had not arrested the top officials of the guild, but Emperor Bindusara had revoked the numerous permits bestowed upon the guild during Emperor Chandragupta's reign. The guild had steadily lost its business contracts in Aryavarta, which included the northern territories of the Mauryan empire. Indrabahu may have been the de facto leader of the guild, but he did not have the authority or charm to hold the once all-powerful organisation together. Ultimately, Ashoka's promises about greater authority being accorded to them was never fulfilled. Further, Bindusara's newly appointed governor was not a puppet like the previous one. He severely curbed the powers of the councillors of the Administrative Council of Gandhara, largely centralising the powers to the one who occupied the Governor's Palace in Takshasila. Bindusara would never allow another rebellion in Gandhara while he was alive. However, with the redundancy of the Administrative Council established, the new governor formed a new de-facto council of erudite advisors from all walks of life. One of these advisors was Haridasa. With the star of several scholars on the rise and the decline of the guild visible, Takshasila was in the grip of change.

Therefore, every merchant decided to extend his influence in north Bharatvarsha on his own, leaving the aegis of the guild behind. Merchant Dhananjaya was already an influential merchant in Gandhara and the territories around the region. Ujjain was one of the major cities well connected to the ports of the western coast of Bharatvarsha. Benefiting from the lucrative trade routes crisscrossing the city was Dhananjaya's goal. Akshaya had already made good progress in the city and was well-known in the city's trade circles. It was from Akshaya that I received the news that Prince Ashoka had been given the governorship of the Avanti Mahajanapada, of which Ujjain was the capital. It was also known that Ujjain was a greater city than Takshasila and was the capital of the central regions of the Mauryan empire.

These two years transformed my life too. My trip to Kalinga with Dharmasena had taken far less time than my journey from Kalinga to Gandhara with the Kalinga Vihara's abbot. Abhaya and Vara were pleased to see me after four long years, but their joy was short-lived. Abhaya had never really gotten over his separation from his brother. When he heard about the death of Udayaditya, he broke down and cried like a little child. Vara was quick to comfort the grieving Abhaya whose tears unceasingly streamed down his face. However, thereafter, Abhaya retreated to a corner of the Vihara, hardly breathing a word. Our pleas eventually brought him out of his corner, but his grief hung around like a miasma, obscuring any hope of reaching his heart. Perhaps, time would heal his wounds and mitigate his sorrow.

With my obligations of relaying the news of Udayaditya's death to Abhaya and the handing over of his ashes fulfilled, it was my turn to be on the receiving end.

The abbot of the Kalinga Vihara was seriously ill. He had lost weight and was not in the right state of mind. When Dharmasena had assured me that the abbot had appeared healthy, his assurances were limited to appearances only. The abbot was incoherent with no understanding of the present situation with a few moments of lucidity at irregular intervals. During the periods of incoherence, he was lost mumbling and recounting his memories of the past. The senior monks of the Vihara were also physicians. However, they were barely able to keep the abbot alive.

"Do you know Dharmasena? It is time we brought Acharya Chanakya back out of retirement. Emperor Bindusara is disconnected from the rest of the Empire. We need the Mamatya to guide the Emperor away from antagonising the southern and northwestern portions of the Empire," he rambled on.

I figured that Abbot Buddhamitra was reliving his days as Lord Dhruva of the Mauryan empire.

"Lord Dhruva, you need to rest. We shall locate the Mamatya and bring him back to Pataliputra. But, we need you to get better for that."

Seeing Dharmasena the abbot calmed down.

"Why did you not share this news with me," I asked Vara. "In Takshasila there are expert physicians who can treat this condition of the Abbot. Why would you keep this from me?"

Vara looked away.

"Before his condition deteriorated, Abbot Buddhamitra made us promise that we would do our best to heal him in the Vihara itself. If we couldn't do anything, we would let him go."

This infuriated me. The abbot, even in this dire situation was making the decisions for the Vihara. I made a decision then and there.

"I am not bound by the promise. I was not at the Vihara when the promise was made. I will do everything in my power to get the best physicians to cure the Abbot. That is my promise to the Vihara."

Fortunately, I had a supporter in Lord Dharmasena. Dharmasena had clout in Pataliputra. He brought the best physicians from the Mauryan capital to cure Abbot Buddhamitra. Over the course of a year, the Mauryan physicians from Pataliputra did their best to cure the abbot. One particular physician named Dhanavantri, named after the God of Physicians himself, brought the abbot out of his delirious state.

The physician, Dhanavantri had once been the royal physician of the Mauryan household. He was an experienced Ayurvedic practitioner who also had a working knowledge of Greek medicine. However, Dhanavantri was one of the several skilled people brought from Takshasila to Pataliputra by Acharya Chanakya when he was still a budding doctor. Therefore, when Chanakya was distanced by Bindusara's administration, Dhanavantri voluntarily distanced himself from the Mauryan household too. However, he harboured a soft spot for Dharmasena because he had a history with Dharmasena's family. Dhanavantri's medical skills and the care heaped upon the abbot by the Sangha helped the abbot recover significantly.

I was at the Vihara when the abbot made his displeasure at my extended stay at the Vihara very clear.

"I do not believe you have achieved exceptional scholarship in any of the known branches of knowledge taught at Takshasila that you languish here at the Vihara, waiting for me to recover."

I grinned back at him, reliving the bygone days of my childhood at the Vihara. After the abbot had concluded his tirade of complaints against me, he found me merrily silent. I thought I saw the shadow of a smile across his face and a tear that rolled down his cheek and was quickly wiped away. We did not need to exchange any more words for our expressions that conveyed everything between us.

Over the next few days, I caught up with Vara, updating him and myself about the latest events in Takshasila and Kalinga respectively. I debated furiously with the abbot on topics I had been taught in Takshasila and the state of the empire as a shift in the power bases appeared on the horizon. I tried cheering up Abhaya, but the man had surrendered himself to grief and was consumed by it. It was as if Lord Kirtimukha had consumed all the joy from his life. The abbot and I heard the teachings of the Buddha discussed among the monks and the nuns teaching the young sramanas about the Tathagata's life. We frequented the Buddhist prayer halls in Kalinga's capital city and the stupas that had newly come up as wealthy patrons liberally opened their purse strings to curry favour with the growing Kalinga Sangha.

However, as the day of my departure drew near, another shock awaited us. The abbot was once again raving like a lunatic, warning us about a plot being hatched to assassinate Acharya Chanakya within the Mauryan palace walls.

"Somebody, anybody there? Acharya's life is in danger. We need to warn him. Send him a message."

The members of the Vihara were dumbfounded as the abbot's mad ramblings continued throughout the night. Fortunately, Dhanavantri had decided to shift his medical practice to the Kalingan capital from Pataliputra. The aged physician was quickly brought to the Vihara. He checked the monk thoroughly and accordingly made him drink a concoction of potent herbs that sedated him and put him to sleep.

The monks and nuns were soon upon the doctor, enquiring about the abbot's condition.

"Whatever is afflicting Lord Buddhamitra is a malady of the mind. Some of the physicians have tried bleeding him to remove the doshas and some have gone as far as suggesting trephination as means of curing his illness. He is reliving his past with renewed vigour while inadvertently neglecting the present. The medicine I have administered is only enough to soothe him. They will bring him only temporary relief. I cannot say if they will bring any long-term curative effects and remedy his condition."

"There must be something we can do, Acharya Dhanavantri," a monk bemoaned."We cannot see him suffer like this. Are these the consequences of his karmic misdeeds performed in his previous birth? There must be a way to ensure his remaining days are spent peacefully."

Dhanavantri understood their unspoken words, but despite his competency, he could not cure the abbot's illness. In fact, he had come across such cases of delirium in his long career as a medicine man, but he did not know of any significant medical breakthroughs which could cure this type of malady.

As the physician walked out of the Vihara, I accosted him while the others fussed over the sleeping monk.

"Acharya, there has to be a way to cure the Abbot's condition. Some remedy which can cure his mind. He was fine yesterday. There is some disease which has afflicted his mind. There has to be a way to restore him to his former self. He cannot live like this. Nobody can."

Dhanavantri gave the question some thought and then answered.

"I believe an improvement in his diet and the medication I have prescribed him shall give him some relief. But, it is only a means to treat his condition. It will not cure him. There may be a way to cure him, but the possible solution may lie elsewhere."

"I do not care if I have to visit the ends of the Earth if I have to find a cure for the Abbot. I saw what loss did to Abhaya. I do not want to be consumed by regret knowing I could have done everything to cure my teacher."

"You do not need to visit the ends of the Earth. There are no ends of the Earth, if it is a Bhugola...sorry, diverted from the topic. The answers may be found in Alexandria.

The physicians of that city are very knowledgeable and treat the study of the human mind as a separate branch of study. This is a very innovative field of study and they may hold the answers behind treating the malady afflicting Abbot Budhamitra. I mention Alexandria because according to Ambassador Deimachus who is a state guest in Pataliputra, the physicians in Alexandria have made some breakthroughs in the field of medical knowledge when it comes to the study of the mind."

I stared back at him and sighed. I had not heard the name Deimachus in two years. Further, I had given up on the dream of travelling to Alexandria, exploring its glorious repositories of knowledge, its centres of enterprise, and culture and interacting with its people. But, Alexandria was not done with me. I shrugged my shoulders. There would have been no harm in living the dream if that had been where fate was leading me. I tried to convince myself it was all for the abbot, but the excitement at having a reason to visit Alexandria told me something.

CHAPTER TWENTY-TWO

ALEXANDRIA CALLS

Dharmasena was in Pataliputra when I informed him about the abbot's deteriorating condition and the possible cure lying in Alexandria. I wanted the Mauryan captain to accompany me on the journey to the Ptolemaic kingdom where Alexandria adorned its northern shores.

Vara and Abhaya took it upon themselves to look after the abbot while expecting help from Pataliputra. Abhaya, despite his great sorrow, went about his duties without a word, leaving no stone unturned in the care of his senior monk. The news of the abbot's deteriorating condition also spread in the neighbouring areas. Influential doctors, merchants and local aristocrats thronged to the Vihara to examine the abbot's condition and enquire about his health.

The majority of the physicians diagnosed him by checking his pulse and declaring that there was an imbalance in the *tridoshas* and *trigunas* i.e. certain biological energies that governed the body and mind and were needed to be in balance for the good health of a person. However, in the abbot's case, his radial pulse told a different story. Dhanavantri had made a similar diagnosis. While treatments were available, there was no certain method to cure the condition.

After a few days, I was surprised to find Dharmasena himself bringing a reply to my message which seemed like a stroke of destiny. Dharmasena and a protective detail of Mauryan soldiers would escort Ambassador Deimachus to Takshasila whose destination coincidentally was Alexandria, to break new ground in the fragile relations between the two great Greek empires of Ptolemy and Antiochus. Soon, the period of the northeast monsoons would be upon the landmass of Bharatvarsha, where powerful and favourable winds would propel both Indian and foreign ships to the sizeable countries that lay in the west across the western sea. Deimachus would be pleased to take the abbot and me to Alexandria and help us in every way possible.

I felt a strange elation knowing the pieces were falling in my favour. The deities of luck were on my side. However, reality soon dampened my enthusiasm when I heard the voice of the abbot as he greeted Dharmasena and enquired about the welfare of his parents. There was no mention of the threats to Acharya Chanakya's life which was all he could think about until a few days ago. There was no mention of the time he had spent as the abbot of the Kalinga Vihara and there was no trace of the Sangha in his memory. It pained me to realise that he had retained his memories of the past when the Vihara where he stood, had been his truth and present for a long time. The abbot and Abhaya were trapped in the throes of their past and we were helpless in its wake.

"Dharmasena, what are we doing here in this Vihara and why am I dressed as a monk," Buddhamitra enquired anxiously.

"Lord Dhruva, Acharya Dhanavantri is here to explain the situation to you."

A look of doubt crossed the abbot's face, as he tried to make sense of this explanation presented to him. Fortunately, Acharya Dhanavantri appeared to our rescue and explained the situation to him. A large grin spread on the abbot's face as he found another face apparently familiar to him other than Dharmasena. I realised that Buddhamitra and Dhanavantri's friendship was another mystery of the abbot's past.

"Lord Dhruva, there was an accident when you were riding your horse to receive visiting dignitaries from the Greek kingdoms. You fell and had a severe concussion. We thought we had lost you when you did not regain consciousness despite our best efforts. It was then that one of the Buddhist monks from Kalinga suggested we bring you here, all the way to Kalinga to heal you. By the efforts and care provided to you by these monks, you are finally conscious and well before us, My Lord. However, you need adequate rest to recover completely, My Lord."

Buddhamitra's eyes widened in shock as he took in this piece of news. He looked at Dharmasena to confirm what he had heard was true and the captain's face confirmed the same.

The abbot was quick to express his gratitude as he individually thanked the monks present for apparently saving his life. The monks were perplexed and hesitantly accepted his gratitude.

While the abbot was going through his ritual of expressing his appreciation, I approached the captain and asked how the physician got the abbot to accept this explanation so easily. A sad smile spread across

Dharmasena's face as he revealed the reason.

"Lord Dhruva was indeed in an accident when he was on his way to receive some important Greek merchants who were invited by Dowager Queen Helena herself during the initial years of Emperor Bindusara's rule. He was unconscious for an entire week. The royal physicians at the Mauryan Court treated him with a variety of remedies, but there were no improvements in his condition. It was then that a group of Buddhist monks volunteered to treat him. After an extensive treatment regimen, Lord Dhruva regained consciousness two days after the treatment started. He recovered quickly enough and regained his health. But..."

"But what...Captain? What happened after that?"

"There was a profound change in his nature. He changed. He suddenly left his position and duties at the Mauryan Court and became a Buddhist monk. Lord Dhruva would not spend another day in Pataliputra after his acceptance of monkhood and he travelled to Kalinga to become a part of this Vihara. It appeared he became...disillusioned. We do not know what happened. He refused to explain this fateful decision that was taken so...unilaterally. He did not consult anybody and never explained his reasons to anyone. Therefore, since this event has happened to him before, I believe his mind readily accepted the explanation provided by Acharya Dhanavantri."

I turned to face Buddhamitra and witnessed the confusion on his face as if he were wracking his head to recall some forgotten memory that seemed just out of reach. For a moment his gaze met mine, but there was no hint of recognition in them. They were empty without any hint of emotion in them. I quickly averted my gaze and retreated from the spot.

I was not there when Dharmasena convinced the abbot that we needed to pay a visit to the distant land of Alexandria, but whatever he stated, Buddhamitra immediately accepted it without question. There was a level of trust which I had never seen the abbot share with anybody else at the Vihara. Perhaps, a part of the abbot still yearned to return to his old life. It pained me

I was in the mango orchard when the abbot also came to sit under a particularly large mango tree. The mango season had ended and the harvests were bountiful this year. However, the trees were capable of providing shade and the abbot who appeared confused, visibly relaxed in the midst of the flora. I did not want to disturb his reverie and decided to leave the spot.

"Do you believe Dhanavantri's reasons for my mental condition," Buddhamitra's voice came, cutting short my escape.

"Excuse me," I stuttered, a feeling of dread rising within me.

"I may have memory problems, but I can read faces. The monks at the Vihara view me as their own and not as a guest whom they have treated and healed. However, for some mysterious reason, the truth is being hidden from me. In fact, I can feel my mind trying to lock away a secret from my knowledge, perceiving it as a threat."

I was taken aback. Buddhamitra continued.

"The truth is that for some reason, I chose to uproot myself and leave my old life behind to settle in the new role of a monk in Kalinga."

"How did you make out all this," I blurted out. The abbot had not only seen through our lies, he had gleaned the truth from our silent faces.

"Why are you telling me all this? You could have discussed this with Lord Dharmasena or Acharya Dhanavantri," I asked cautiously.

"They are the men who gave me an answer to my questions. But, you are the man who will help me seek the answers to my questions."

"But...Dhanavantri said," I stammered

"Dhanavantri informed me that there are plans to take a trip to Alexandria to escort Ambassador Deimachus, who is the State Guest in Pataliputra. I am assuming this is tied to finding answers to remedy my condition. If I can make the trip to Takshasila with you to make your future, you can make a trip with me to Alexandria to figure out my past."

Epilogue

As the *Thalassa*, a weather-beaten Greek ship arrived at the newly constructed port of Myos Hormos, its once-glistening green hull was storm-eroded and salt-stained with its proud sails in tatters. The majestic figurehead at the bow, a deity meant to protect the ship against the perils of the sea, appeared grateful that her weary vigil had ended with the arduous journey. The ship's rigging was worn out with frayed ropes and rusted chains. The ship had endured months of battering and bruising at the hands of the monsoon winds and choppy waters with much of its precious cargo of spices, ivory and precious stones intact.

However, it was the crew's dogged resistance that had paid off. As the ship docked at the harbour, the haggard men were already engaged in the process of repairing the ship for any damage and unloading its precious cargo from the cargo hold.

While the passengers made their way from the ship to the customs houses and then onto the nearby inns and guesthouses, a hooded figure with two trusted and loyal servants carrying all his earthly possessions made his way to a run-down guesthouse of obscure repute. Once he had settled down, he sent a servant with an encrypted message to an associate of his in the port city. The message contained details of an invitation for a meeting at a particular place of disrepute. The place was an inn, a den frequented by thieves, smugglers, mercenaries and assassins, each with sordid tales to their name.

The hooded passenger's associate was the first one to arrive and seated himself in a dim corner of the inn, a respectable merchant in the guise of a ruffian whose mannerisms indicated that despite his garb, he was unaccustomed to these notorious surroundings. The man in the hood soon made his way to the corner and greeted his associate politely.

"Hello, Castor," the man politely addressed the Greek merchant in a hushed voice.

"My friend, it has been a while," the Greek merchant rose to greet his addressor.

Both men took their respective seats and exchanged pleasantries and immediately got down to business.

"Castor, how are your relations with the Royal Household?"

"My wife Sophia remains a close friend of Queen Arsinoe and has her ear. But, I cannot promise unchecked access to royal patronage."

"I do not need patronage. All I need are one or two favours. As and when the time comes, I will call upon you to deliver these favours from the Royal Household. If I win, I can promise great rewards and riches await you."

Castor gave the proposal some thought.

"I do not want riches, my friend. I want power," Castor remarked boldly.

The man in the hood took note of the sudden change in the tone of his associate.

"What power do you wish you for, Castor."

"I estimated how great a favour you needed when you appeared personally in my city to demand the favour and when you asked me how close I was to the Royal Household of Egypt. These favours from the Royal Household do not come cheap. Riches can be obtained through commerce and trade with India which is very lucrative. But merchants do not come across power until we have royal patronage. While you may not seek royal patronage from Pharaoh

Ptolemy, I seek royal patronage from the future emperor of India."

A smile played out on the face of the hooded figure. He had approached the right man who had read the situation immediately from his words. As long as the price of the favour was met, the agreement was executable without morality and ethics proving obstacles.

"If you get me my favour, I will have the future emperor of India grant you the rights to establish a permanent settlement in Barygaza. You will have access to the premier port on the western coast of the country with legal protection, reduced customs duties and tax exemptions, land rights to establish warehouses and markets and even a monopoly on certain goods imported into the country."

Castor raised an eyebrow as he heard the promises made by the man he addressed as a friend.

"You can deliver all this if I deliver from my end?"

"Yes, but only if the favour is delivered."

"It will be delivered and if you need a tacit royal order for the Pharaoh of Egypt, you need to travel with me to Alexandria to find the Shadow of Ra. Sophia will do the rest to convince Queen Arsinoe."

"Good, then it is settled. We leave first thing in the morning."

"Are you certain, my friend? Think again. If you set this in motion, it will lead to fatal consequences."

The hooded figure revealed his face to the horror of his Greek associate.

"Vasunaga, what happened to your face?"

The refugee merchant from Gandhara stood one-eyed. In the place of his left eye, a hollow socket was there with slight scarring on the skin around the socket and a long scar running from his brow to his cheek.

"This is punishable by death and the events I am going to set in motion will be catastrophic for my enemies. The Shadow of Ra will assassinate Ashoka of the Maurya dynasty and I will have my vengeance. Everything was business for me, but this..." he said pointing at the loss of his left eye, "...is personal for me."